Under the Gun in Brooklyn

An Eddie Lombardi Mystery

Douglas DiNunzio

BookLocker
Saint Petersburg, Florida

Published by BookLocker.com, Inc., St. Petersburg, Florida.

Printed on acid-free paper.

The characters and events in this book are fictitious. Any similarity to real persons, living or dead, is coincidental and not intended by the author.

BookLocker.com, Inc.
2020

First Edition

For Jean

"Commit a crime, and the earth is made of glass."
                    -- Ralph Waldo Emerson

1

I should never have gone out that morning. First, the weather was vile. It was April, mid-April if you want to know, but outside my new house on 16th Avenue in Bensonhurst, Borough of Brooklyn, it was sleeting. There were patches of black ice on the streets and sidewalks wherever the sleet had changed to freezing rain, and the temperature was hovering in the mid-thirties. A malevolent wind was blowing, too, one of those wild, apocalyptic winds that you hear about from time to time in church on Sunday mornings, especially if you've got an excitable parish priest telling you about it, and if you can hear the damn thing blowing like a hurricane against the stained glass. If you listen to our parish priest, Father Giacomo, long enough, he'll convince you that the Four Horsemen of the Apocalypse are double-parked in a hearse on New Utrecht Avenue, just waiting to crash the service.

In this kind of weather, or any kind, I would've chanced taking the car, due to the fact that my *goombah* Gino's supermarket was several long blocks away and my delicate Eye-talian feet were missing four toes thanks to frostbite in the Battle of the Bulge. But the car was in the shop -- again -- and so I was on foot in this freezing downpour, without an umbrella or a prayer. Not that either would have helped much.

Except for the weather, all this unpleasantness was my wife Laura's doing. She'd made me trade away my reliable Chevy for a Chrysler station wagon that wouldn't start. The car didn't need repair, just a priest to say the Last Rites over it after the exorcisms had failed. Laura's argument had been that we were a growing family and therefore needed what was politely known as a "family" car. Not to mention that her younger brother Johnny Temafonte assembled Chryslers in Detroit. And so I was walking to the supermarket in the freezing rain and cyclonic wind for nothing more than a loaf of bread, a bottle of whole milk, and a tube of toothpaste. Wife's orders.

I passed a newsstand on the way and glanced at the headlines. Yuri Gagarin, the Russian cosmonaut, had just orbited the earth. Adolf Eichmann was in the dock in Israel, on trial for war crimes. The usual local news was on the inside pages if I'd cared to look -- society scandals, crime, births and deaths -- but I wasn't much interested in the news these days, not even the sports news. The Brooklyn Dodgers were in Los Angeles now, and Ebbets Field had fallen under the wrecking ball only last year. With the Flock gone, there wasn't much to cheer about in the Borough of Brooklyn, even in the best weather.

I was still blocks away from Gino's market, fighting the stiff wind and trying to keep from slipping and breaking my Eye-talian neck on the black ice, when the big black Pontiac pulled up and two goons stepped out just ahead of me. Given my dark mood, and the weather, I wouldn't have stopped if the Virgin Mary in pink toreador pants and a wig hat had called out to me; but in Brooklyn, when guys like that block the sidewalk, you stop walking and give them some attention.

"Well, good morning," I said amiably. "Are you fellows on your way to church? You could pass for altar boys."

"Get in the car, Lombardi," one of them said. They were lean and tall, and they wore slick black raincoats that went all the way down to their black shoe tops. Rainwater dripped off their black fedoras, which were pulled low over their eyes. If they had faces, I couldn't see them through the rain.

"And why should I do that?" I asked, which must have made them smile.

"Just get in the car," said the second goon. I eyeballed them for a moment, strictly out of habit, but they were not to be turned away. The one who'd spoken first slipped his hand into the deep pocket of his raincoat. Shamelessly, and somewhat carelessly, I grinned at him.

"Is that a .38 in there, or are you just happy to see me?" I said, ramping up the grin.

He pointed to the open back door of the Pontiac. I smiled again, less boldly, and took my place between him and his lethal twin on the back seat. The driver, a stocky, taciturn fellow, didn't turn around. It was a tight fit on that back seat, even for a full-sized Pontiac, and I could feel cold steel through wet fabric pushing hard against my kidneys. The hood on my left tapped the driver on his shoulder, and the big black Pontiac pulled away from the curb.

"Are we going somewhere?" I asked in my best deadpan.

"You'll find out," said the one on my right. He had a deeper voice, so I assumed he was in charge.

"Oh, it'll be a surprise then. I like surprises, don't you? Like those decoder rings in cereal boxes."

"A comedian," he said brusquely to the other. But they must have liked the joke, because the pressure of the two gun barrels against my kidneys eased a bit. I used that small but hopeful development to push the joke a bit further.

"Wherever we're going, would you fellows mind stopping at the market first? Got to pick up a few things for the wife."

Nobody answered.

"She'll be properly pissed if I don't pick them up. Seriously. Are you guys married? Not to *each other*, I mean. It's just that, if you were, you'd understand my situation a little better. Hell hath no fury like the little woman who..."

"You talk too much," said the goon on my left. "Why don't you just shut up?"

"No, seriously," I said. "I've got some important shopping to do, and you fellows are keeping me from it."

"Are we gonna have to keep listenin' to this guy?" said the goon on my left. The driver kept silent.

"Just shut up till we get there, Lombardi," said the other goon.

"Get where?"

"You'll see."

"I'll see, right. You said that already, didn't you? So, who do you fine fellows work for?"

"The boss."

9

"Right. Of course. Dumb question."

"Can you maybe shut up now?"

I pointed out the window. "There's the market," I said. "Pull over. Only take a minute. Three little items, that's all."

Again, nobody answered, the barrels of the .38s dug into my kidneys again, and we drove on.

I took a moment to try to remember the last time I'd been taken for a ride by hoods like these. It was back in '49. My not-so-gentle kidnappers were a pair of no-necks I called Superman and Calamari Breath for reasons that aren't worth the time or effort it would take to explain. They belonged to a *capo* named Alberto Scarpetti. Alberto was having some trouble with the District Attorney's Office and was hoping I'd find a way to get him out of it. He eventually got to ride the Sparky up in Sing Sing, which should give you some idea of how much help I was to him. No, it wouldn't be Alberto Scarpetti who'd be hosting whatever little soiree these two hoods were planning for me, but he was of the same ilk.

I paid some attention now to which direction we were driving. We were headed south along New Utrecht Avenue, which could mean any number of familiar places: Gravesend, Coney Island, Sheepshead Bay, Gerritsen Beach, Floyd Bennett Field. And if you traveled further east from there, along Shore Parkway, there was Canarsie, East New York, Ozone Park, and Howard Beach. I was hoping our destination wasn't going to be Floyd Bennett Field, because that's where the Mob was rumored to dispose of its most undesirable undesirables. There were enough wetlands, bogs, and tidal swamps around Floyd Bennett Field to hide a regiment of decomposing stiffs. If you believed the rumors, there were almost as many graves there, albeit unmarked, as in Green-Wood Cemetery, where many of Brooklyn's most famous swells and not-so-swells were planted.

So I asked, "Okay. Where *are* we going, and who *is* your boss?" When I received the same cold silence, I added, "My wife is really going to be pissed when I don't come home with the groceries, but then I already told you that."

"That's all taken care of," said the hood on my left.

"*Taken care of?*"

"That's right."

"So, does that mean *you're* going to buy the groceries?" I asked, almost seriously.

"You know what we mean," said the goon on my right.

"No, I *don't*," I said. "That's why I'm asking the question. And what's my wife got to do with this, whatever *this* is? What the hell has *she* done?"

Neither goon answered. That made me nervous.

"Does this have anything to do with my business? Because if it does, my wife is my office secretary, and that's all. I don't tell her anything that she doesn't need to know about anything or anybody, okay?" It was a lie, but a believable one, or so I hoped.

"Lighten up, Lombardi," said the hood on my left, just as the hood on my right shifted his weight ever so slightly and the heft of his handgun pressed that much harder into my side.

"Well, you can just leave my wife out of this," I continued, feeling a little of the *agita* now. "It's bad enough I'm going to catch hell from her about the groceries. You leave her out of it, *capisce?*" It was weak, ill-timed bravado at best, and I caught laughter from both goons, so I decided to shut up again.

I felt some relief when we passed Floyd Bennett Field, still moving due east, but then a new thought struck me. Maybe the cemetery at Floyd Bennett was already filled, and they were going to dump my bullet-riddled Eye-talian body somewhere else. I remembered a case back in '55 when a duck pond out on Long Island had served that grim purpose. But that Potter's Field of nameless dead had been shut down for good, thanks to me, my hotheaded partner Arnie Pulaski, and several squads of New York's Finest. The thought was comforting, but only for a moment. Maybe there was another duck pond out there somewhere, just waiting for me. Maybe I was going to be its very first tenant. But for doing exactly what?

We skirted north of Jamaica Bay and continued east into Long Island. When we kept going in that direction on the Southern State Parkway, far from the comforting confines of Kings County, I felt real panic for the first time. The goon on my left took notice of my concern and smiled, almost benevolently.

"Still haven't figured it out, have you, Lombardi? Where you're goin', who you're gonna see."

"You might say that," I answered. I glanced past him out the window. It was sleeting again, harder. The big Pontiac moved almost snake-like along the flooded parkway, floating on the slick surface, just short of hydroplaning.

"I told you not to sweat it," said the goon again. "Told you to lighten up, didn't I?"

"You did, yes," I said. "You might also tell your driver to slow down, if you don't mind. I've got a wife and kids, as you know. She won't be a merry widow if your *cafone* of a driver skids this loose cannon of a car into a tree."

"Relax," said the other hood. "You're too tense. It ain't healthy to be so tense."

"Maybe I've got a good reason," I said. I didn't want to give them ideas, but I wanted answers instead of evasion.

"Well, if you really gotta know, I suppose we can tell you. We're goin' to the Jones Beach Hotel out in Wantaugh. The boss, he's booked a room there. He wants to talk to you, that's all."

"*In Wantaugh? In this weather?*"

"His idea, Lombardi. Like I said. He just wants to talk to you about somethin', that's all. Don't sweat it."

"Oh, I see. That's just swell. And for the last time, who exactly *is* your boss?"

"Mr. Santini."

I turned to look at the goon on my right. His large, toothy smile had grown larger. "Surprised, Lombardi?" he said.

For a while, I sat silently between the two hoods, pondering the imponderable and deciding what to say in my final prayers. Jimmy Santini was the biggest mob boss in Brooklyn, and had been for fifteen years or more. He was a bona fide stone killer. I hadn't had any serious contact with him since the Scarpetti business back in '49 and an earlier encounter in '47, and I didn't want to have any serious contact with him now. He lived in Gravesend, on a large, gated estate protected by a small army of goons like these two, plus guard dogs and an electrified fence. What the hell was he doing meeting a shamus in a tourist hotel way out on Long Island?

"I still don't get it," I said.

"Too bad," said the goon on my right. "But that's where we're goin'."

"What does Santini want with me?" I asked. "I barely know the guy."

"*Mr.* Santini," said the goon on my right.

"Just take it easy," said the goon on my left. "Honest to God, nothin's gonna happen."

"Nothin' at all."

"Oh yeah? Well..."

"*Jesus Christ! Cut the shit, Lombardi! Nothin' bad's gonna happen to ya, unless ya keep flappin' your goddamn gums!* " It was the driver's voice that I heard this time. I would've had a snappy comeback, but I kept silent because it was a voice that I recognized, even after fourteen years.

The voice of Mr. James Santini, mobster.

2

He was out of the car, walking through the sleet and into the Jones Beach Hotel, but his goons wouldn't let me out of the black Pontiac. I had the feeling that he was in a hurry -- that they were all in a hurry -- and not on account of the weather. For a moment, as he disappeared into the lobby, I thought about my wife Laura and my two little girls, the older of whom would be at school now. Laura would worry when I didn't return from the market, but there wasn't anything I could do about that. All I could do was to consider present circumstances and steel myself against the worst possibilities, any and all of which could be lethal.

While I waited in the car with Santini's goons, I took some time to check out the hotel. It had three floors, with a restaurant at ground level. The hotel was small and unremarkable, constructed of unpainted brick. The restaurant was in the *faux*-Tudor style. Neither establishment would earn five stars, but they were the best that could be had this close to Jones Beach. There was no hotel of any kind at the beach. Robert Moses, who'd designed the place mostly for his wealthy friends in and out of New York State government, had seen to that. His nice little beach was not for the hoi polloi or cheap tourist hotels.

After sitting and waiting for a while in the Pontiac, one of the goons said, "All right, Lombardi. Inside."

The room was on the third floor, looking south toward the beach. But you couldn't see the beach from there. Even if the sky had been clear, you couldn't see it. It was miles away. One of the goons brought me to a door and knocked twice. A voice inside -- Jimmy Santini's voice -- said loudly, commandingly, "Okay. Now, go and wait in the car." The door to the room swung open, the goon retreated, and I stepped cautiously past the threshold. The lights were out. There were blackout curtains on the windows, and they had been drawn shut. "Over here," said Santini, and I moved in the direction of his voice. As I approached, I saw his dim outline in the corner. Then a table lamp turned on and I saw him, still dimly, his face still in shadow, dressed in a plain dark suit. A cheap, wet raincoat hung over the back of a chair. Santini was known around the Five Boroughs as a flashy dresser, so the look surprised me. There was another chair across from him in front of the darkened window. I was expected to sit in it, but at the moment I preferred to stand.

"Sit down, Lombardi," he said pleasantly, pointing at it. "Take a load off." I sat. I took in the image of him for a moment. I hadn't seen him in the flesh since '47, but he looked unchanged. The same heft, the same bulldog face, the same bold carriage. He'd always held himself well, always presented the perfect picture of a *don*, a *capo*, a boss among bosses. It wasn't until I gave him a more studied look that I noticed he was scowling at me.

"So, you don't like my driving, huh? There's something wrong with my driving?"

"Your driving's...fine," I said.

"You said I was a *cafone*. That's what you said. You think maybe I'm some kind of fool, is that it?"

"I didn't realize it was you, Mr. Santini. And I had a few other things on my mind when I said it."

"I'm a good driver, damn good driver, if you wanna know. In thirty-five years, not a single ticket. Not one. Of course, most of the time, the boys, they take me where I wanna go, and if *they* get a ticket, I get it fixed."

"But they're not driving today," I said. "How come?"

"I like to drive. Relaxes me, helps me think. Main thing is, here we are, and nobody but us and my boys outside knows it. Besides, my chauffeur, he's takin' the wife to the beauty parlor or someplace."

"All right," I said. "So, here we are. But why?"

"We'll be gettin' to that," he said, and lit a cigarette. The case it came from looked like platinum. He smoked for a moment, drawing deep on it, disconnected, remote, as if he somehow thought himself alone in the room. I almost expected him to pick his nose or give some attention to his crotch. But then he looked at me and said, "I'd offer one, but I know you don't smoke. You drink, but only beer, and only Schaefer. You're honest, you're dependable, and you can handle yourself in a tight spot. You fought in the war, in the Airborne. You got a Purple Heart and some combat medals on D-Day. You go to church every Sunday with your wife and two kids. You're one of those straight-arrow types, sure, but you're not perfect. You don't play so nice with the guys who are married to your three kid sisters, and you hang around sometimes with a big spook from up in Harlem, which is not very Eye-talian. That's the word on you, anyway. See, I did some research."

"Good for you," I said. "You expecting a prize or something?" I was ridiculing one of the most dangerous men in the Five Boroughs, but I didn't care at the moment. I was tired of playing whatever game this was, regardless of the consequences. Oddly, he didn't react, and I wondered if he'd even heard me.

"I need a guy like that right about now," he said. "I need a guy like you, Lombardi."

Now I was the one who wasn't sure what he'd heard. "You want *me* to work for *you*? Mr. Santini, with all due respect..."

"Just for a while, maybe. A special job. All legal and upright. Nothin' to fuss about." He flicked some cigarette ash into an ashtray on the small table next to his chair.

"Mr. Santini..."

"Call me Jimmy. We're gonna be great pals. I just know it."

"Mr. Santini, with all due respect..."

"And cut out this 'respect' shit. I just gave you permission to call me Jimmy. Get it? Jimmy. *Jih-mee.* Two fuckin' syllables. You can handle a couple of syllables, can't you, Lombardi?"

"This work, this job you're talking about, what would it be? If you don't mind my asking."

"*Mind*? Why would I *mind*? What the fuck you think I brought you all the way out here for?"

"That's the other question," I said. "Why here? Why not just see me at my office? Or at your home? Why here?"

"Secrecy, Lombardi. Secrecy. Besides, I sort of own this place."

"Sort of?"

"You know –- silent partner. That kind of thing. Helps out with the taxes."

"And the blackout curtains...?"

"Like I said, secrecy. Security. Jesus Christ. Am I gonna have to say everything *twice* to you?"

"All right, I'm listening. What's the work?"

"Somebody wants to kill me."

I was so busy trying to suppress the grin that was coming that I just stared at him. The grin poked through anyway.

"What's so funny?"

"With all due respect..."

"I told you to cut out that 'respect' shit."

"What I meant to say was, considering your particular line of work, shouldn't that be a given?"

"I'm not talkin' about competitors, Lombardi. Besides, none of them would have the balls to try. I'm talkin' closer to home. A lot closer."

"Who do you think wants to kill you?"

"I don't fuckin' know. If I did, he –- or she –- would be fuckin' dead by now. You know what they say: do unto others what they wanna do to you, but do it first."

"All right," I said. "How do you know that somebody 'close to home,' as you put it, wants to kill you?"

He smiled his best mobster smile. "A little bird told me."

I stood up. "I was hoping this might turn into a serious conversation," I said, frowning. "You're not helping much."

"I just know, that's all," he said stiffly. "Sit down."

"You know, but you *don't* know?" I asked, pulling the chair away a good distance before complying.

"I don't know who, I don't know why, and I don't know when. But I know. I *know*, okay?"

"And my job is...?"

"To find out who before they do what they're plannin' on doin' sometime soon. Got that much?"

"All right. So, who do you suspect?"

"You want the list in alphabetical order, maybe? Or by age? Males first? Females first? You call it, Lombardi."

"Anyway you like. How many people are we talking about?"

He glanced at his cigarette, which had burned down to the filter. He dropped it into the ashtray. "Seven," he said.

"*Seven* people?"

"There you go again. I gotta say everything twice to you?"

"Okay, just the names, then."

"You gonna take notes?"

"Not necessary," I said, trying not to grin while lying through my teeth. "I'm told I have a photographic memory."

"Okay, first there's my bitchy wife Wanda, and then there's my daughter Maria, and my daughter's shrink, and my lawyer, and my chauffeur, and my two boys."

"Carmine and Rico? The Barracuda Brothers?"

"That's the two boys, right. I think you know 'em."

I did, indeed, and the daughter, too, but there was no point in asking why about any of it. All I wanted to do now was walk out of the room. I'd hitchhike all the way back to Bensonhurst if necessary, but I didn't want to be in Santini's company a moment longer. If he read the pained expression on my face, he didn't show it. He continued. "What I want you to do, on the quiet, naturally, is to keep an eye on all of 'em, see what they're up to. Couple of times a week, I'll call your office from a pay phone, and you can tell me what you found out."

"Mr. Santini..."

"Jimmy, remember? *Jih-mee*. Two syllables."

"Tell me again, if you don't mind, why *these* seven people? Why not anybody else?"

"If I could explain it, I'd explain it. I'll tell you again. One, or more than one, of those seven people, they want me dead, and soon. I just know it, that's all. What's the word for that? Inquisition?"

"Intuition, but..."

"So, I'm hiring you, and that's that."

"Mr. Santini..."

"*Jih-mee.*"

"What I'm trying to say is, it won't work."

"And why not?"

"I only have one junior partner, and two associates who are available to me *at times.* I don't have nearly enough resources to do the job you want done."

"Then hire some more people."

"Let me explain something to you," I said, almost desperate in my frustration. "Surveillance operations are usually done in eight-hour shifts. That means I'd need *three men* to keep tabs on *each* of the seven people you want followed, if you want it done right. That's twenty-one different operatives for any given twenty-four-hour surveillance, seven days a week. Anything less than that, and I can't offer any guarantees."

"So, just do the best you can with whoever you can get," said Santini. "There's five grand in it for you. Split it up with your guys any way you like."

"Wait a minute now..."

"No excuses, Lombardi. You get half now, half when you give me the names and the proof. Unless, of course, they get me first."

"They?"

"Could be one of 'em, could be two, could be all seven together. That's for you to figure out, Lombardi." He reached over and pulled a fat wad of bills from inside the pocket of his raincoat, which was still dripping onto the carpet. He tried to hand it to me, but I didn't take it.

"You seem to think you've got some kind of a choice here," he said, frowning, still holding out the money.

"Don't I?"

"Your first choice -- you takin' the money, you doin' the job for me -- now that's a good choice. A real good choice. A smart choice. You *not* takin' the money, after everything I just told you, that means you know some stuff about me that maybe you shouldn't. That means I can't trust you. That means maybe I gotta do somethin' that I don't really wanna do, although it'll be those two guys outside who'll be doin' it. But I'm not totally heartless. I'd make sure your wife got the five grand. There'd be no proper funeral, naturally, with you disappearin' all sudden like, and the money would have to get to her anonymous-like, but you got nothin' to worry about, as far as that goes."

He was still holding out the money, and I still wasn't taking it. I was in the midst of an unusual reverie at the moment, recalling a similar discussion I'd had with the late Alberto Scarpetti in '49. It was sleeting now. It had been snowing then. The offer had been twice what Santini was offering me: ten thousand dollars; but the punishment for saying 'no' was exactly the same. I was in a box of sorts, and we both knew it. I didn't want to end up in another kind of box, not that they'd bother to plant me in one. More likely, the bottom of another duck pond or a shallow grave over by Floyd Bennett Field.

"Let me make sure I understand this," I said, as calmly as I could. "You want me and my operatives to tail *seven* people for an indeterminate amount of time because you *imagine* one or more of them wants to kill you, and the offer is only five grand?"

"All right," he said. "Make it ten."

"You're *sure* you want to do this?" I asked. He took another wad from the pocket of his plain suit jacket, counted the bills carefully, and held the money out. I took it, finally, and tucked it away in my raincoat pocket.

Santini stood up from his chair, walked casually to the window that faced Jones Beach, and raised the shade.

"Well, that's done," he said, smiling amiably. "I bet you're glad I did that."

"Did what?"

"Raised the shade. You oughta be, you know. Another couple of minutes of you sayin' 'no,' and..."

"It's still sleeting outside," I said, pretending to miss his point.

"No it ain't, Lombardi. It's a swell day, and don't you forget it," he said without a smile. He walked to the door and opened it. "Don't you forget it for a minute. You understand?"

"Yes," I said. "I understand."

"Every once in a while, I gotta do some not-so-nice things to people," he said in a voice that almost approached contrition. "Usually they're not-so-nice people, so it don't matter that much. But it ain't always that way. I don't wanna do those kind of things to you, Lombardi. Understand? Not that I wouldn't if you didn't give me no other choice, but I wouldn't feel so good about it. Anyway, this is better. Now we're pals, and everything's swell. That's how I like it. Do *you* like it?"

"Of course, Mr. Santini."

"Jih-mee. Okay?"

"Jimmy. Sure."

He smiled. "So. That wasn't so bad, was it?"

"It was fine," I said.

"We can drive back now. Back to Brooklyn. You can pick up those groceries you were bitchin' about."

"And my wife?"

"Your wife is fine, Lombardi. She's just fine. And those two little girls, they're both fine. You trust me, right?"

"I guess I have to."

"Don't sweat it. And remember. I'll be callin' you every coupla days. And I'm gonna be expectin' some progress."

"I'll do the best I can," I said.

"No, Lombardi. You're gonna do *better* than your best. And so are the guys who are gonna work for you."

"All right."

"I always liked you, Lombardi. You know that? Always liked you. Gonna like you even more if and when you do right by me."

"And your money," I said.

"Yeah. And my money."

"Would you care to make it fifteen?" I asked with a little boy look.

"Ten," he said. "Come on. The car's waitin'."

"And who's driving?"

He smiled. "I am, Lombardi. The *cafone*'s gonna be at the wheel."

3

He dropped me a block away from my house, and I walked the rest of the way through a light rain. Laura was waiting for me on the front stoop, under a large, dripping black umbrella. Her face was set in a hard scowl. Rather than have the argument I knew was coming in public, I walked past her and waited for her to follow. I stopped in the kitchen.

"I can explain," I said when we were both inside.

"*Explain?*"

"Laura..."

"There were *men* here, Eddie. *Men. Thugs.* In our *house.* In the place where our *children* sleep."

"You weren't in any danger," I said, and right away I wished I hadn't said it.

"Oh, no?"

"Seriously. They weren't here to hurt you."

"And who told you that?"

"The man who sent them," I said. "Jimmy Santini."

"The *mobster?*"

"Yes."

"And what in God's name does Jimmy Santini the mobster have to do with *you?* With *us?* With this *family?*"

"He wants me to work for him. Surveillance job. That's all."

"That's *all?* The biggest mobster in Brooklyn wants to hire you, and you say that's *all?*"

"I didn't say it was okay, Laura..."

"Thank God Amanda was at school when those men came. Thank God our little Mary was still asleep in her bedroom. The hoods, they sat *right there*, the two of them," she said, pointing furiously at the kitchen table. "*Right there!*"

"Laura..."

"So, this mobster, he actually *spoke* to you?"

"Yes."

"In person?"

"Yes."

"Where?"

"A hotel out on Long Island. Laura…"

"Well, you told him 'no,' didn't you? I certainly hope you told him. You *did*, didn't you?"

I pulled the still-damp wad of money from the pocket of my raincoat and dropped it unceremoniously on the kitchen table. "'No' wasn't an option, Laura," I said, and waited for the gale to break over me. But she only gasped and covered her mouth with trembling hands. "It'll be all right, really," I said, but she ran into the bedroom in tears and slammed the door behind her. I figured she was through reviling me for the moment, but then the door re-opened.

"And will you please get the groceries now?" she shouted, and slammed the door again.

I was still trying to figure out what steamroller had run over me when I walked into Gino's supermarket. Once the self-appointed ombudsman of the neighborhood, Gino had been less active in that capacity since he joined the Moose Lodge about a year back. I kidded him about it as often as I could, sometimes referring to it as the Mystic Knights of the Sea from *Amos and Andy* or the Raccoon Lodge from *The Honeymooners*, but really I was just happy that he'd found another outlet for his obsessive civic-mindedness and general meddling. And I was even happier that he no longer sought out *pro bono* cases for me. It was a *pro bono* case he'd shackled me with back in '49 that introduced me to my future partner, Arnie Pulaski. Arnie was in the running to win Juvenile Delinquent of the Year when we'd first met, with a murder charge on him that I was seriously hoping would stick. How Arnie went from teenage terror to my detecting alter ego is a story too complicated to go into here. Suffice it to say that Arnie and I have had our ups and downs, and almost as many falling outs as I've had with Gino.

One of Gino's five teen-aged kids was usually stationed at the checkout when I showed up, but this time it was Gino himself, front and center, and acting as if all the known universe revolved around him and his fresh produce. He'd put on a few pounds, all in the belly, since I'd last seen him, but it was better not to mention that.

"Don't ask," I said when he gave me that look that says, "I know you've got trouble, so what is it?"

"So, what is it?" he asked anyway.

"Rough morning," I said. "And it isn't over yet."

"Laura's pissed at you?"

"With good reason."

"Nothin' new there," he said, and semi-smiled at me. "So, you just came in to whine about your rough morning, or you got a reason to be here?"

It occurred to me that I'd forgotten what I was supposed to pick up. Three small items, and I couldn't remember even one of them. Given Laura's current mood, I was in no position to call home and ask for clarification, so I just gave Gino a dumb look. "It'll come to me," I said.

"Well, I was gonna call you anyway," he said, as his smile turned serious. Never a good sign, that.

"Oh, please, not another..."

"No, no," he said. "It's a family thing. I need some help with a family thing, that's all."

I already had a family thing going -- with Jimmy Santini's family -- but I couldn't tell Gino that. So I pretended to listen while I tried to remember those three items that I had to bring home or suffer the consequences.

"You ever hear of beatniks?" he asked suddenly.

"Beatniks?" I parroted back.

"That's what they call 'em."

"Okay."

"Does that mean you know what I'm talkin' about?"

"Probably not," I said. "I've heard the word, anyway."

"They're oddballs. They talk funny, they dress funny, they *look* funny. They're not like us. They're part of what's known these days as the 'current generation.' Jesus! Whatever happened to civilization, anyway?"

"Beats me. And?"

"One of 'em's lookin' a little too close at my little girl Gloria, that's what."

"So, how old is she now?"

"Old enough to know better."

"These college kids," I said. "What can you do?"

"Well, she's been hangin' around with them, and this one guy in particular. Wears a beret, don't bathe, spouts poetry that don't rhyme. And I'm bettin' he smokes that marijuana stuff and don't change his underwear."

"She's a big girl," I said.

"That don't make her wise to the ways of the world, Eddie," he said, frowning now. "Don't make her know what she oughta be knowin' 'bout beatniks and similar kinds of undesirables."

"And I'm supposed to do exactly what?"

"Follow her for a coupla days. Keep an eye on her. Her and her weird boyfriend. She's up at NYU."

"No can do, Gino," I said. I couldn't tell him that I didn't have a spare second in the foreseeable future and beyond, and I certainly couldn't tell him the reason why.

"I'll pay you," he said.

"No can do," I insisted. "I'm booked solid on another case."

"What case?"

"I'm not at liberty to say," I said stiffly, and suddenly two of the three things I had to pick up popped into my head.

"Now, listen here, Eddie..."

"Bread and milk!" I said with some excitement. "I came here to get bread and milk... and something else. Damned if I can remember what it was." I left him open-mouthed at the checkout and raced up one of the aisles. When I found what I was looking for, I returned to the checkout. Maybe Laura would go easier on me if I remembered two of the three, but probably not. So my mind was still disengaged when Gino brought up the subject of beatniks and his daughter again.

"Could you at least try to talk some sense into her?" he said, just short of imploring me.

"About what?"

"Beatniks, of course. And why she'd do better with a nice Italian boy, like the ones on *American Bandstand*."

"I don't know a thing about beatniks, or poets, or folk singers, or any of those kinds of people," I argued. "And what makes you think that *you* do?"

"She *told* me, of course. She's been braggin' about this guy, and about what she calls the Beat Generation. You ever heard of some poet named Ginsberg?"

"Can't say I have."

"She started readin' me one of his poems the other day. Jesus! One fuckin' dirty word after another! That asshole's mind is in the fuckin' sewer! Jesus H. Christ!"

"Like I said, she's a big girl. I bet she's already familiar with those words, and a few more."

"Beat Generation, huh? Well, I'll make sure her little Eye-talian behind is part of the *beat* generation if I ever find her foolin' around with some unwashed beatnik."

"It's none of my business, Gino, even if I had the time, which I don't."

"Come on, Eddie," he pleaded. "Do me a goddamn favor."

I smiled. "I thought you said you were going to pay me."

"Okay, okay. I'll pay you."

"I don't have the time, Gino. Swear to God I don't."

"Okay, okay. Just talk to her, then."

"*When I have the time*," I said. "And after I learn a thing or two about beatniks."

"Okay, okay."

"And I can't even say when I'll be able to do it."

"Okay. But you *will* do it?"

I was looking straight at him, but my mind was elsewhere again. "Toothpaste!" I shouted, and raced up the aisle.

4

I hurried home, put the milk bottle in the refrigerator, the bread in the breadbox, and the toothpaste in the bathroom. Then I left before Laura could find another fatal flaw in my character to dwell on. There were times in our married life when it was better to be anywhere but home, and this was one of them.

I had an office over the Bella Italia Luncheonette on 18th Avenue, from where I usually conducted business. But before I could go there, I decided to look up my sometime favorite snitch, Aurelio Rodriguez. That meant getting the Chrysler back from the repair shop on New Utrecht. Only last year Aurelio had threatened to die on me, but he'd survived his chronic alcoholism somehow and was still getting around. I'd been told that he was a teetotaler these days, but since bars had always given him a special kind of solace, he could still be found in one. I went looking in all the usual places -- Nero's, The Tip Top Tavern, the local bowling alleys -- but it wasn't until I got to Winky's across from the Alcoholics Anonymous location on 99th Street in Queens that I finally found him. He was sitting alone in a dark corner booth scowling fiercely and nursing a 7-Up. His beverage of choice before that had been J.T.S. Brown, fine Kentucky bourbon, which he'd often accepted as legal tender in lieu of cash.

"*Hola*, Aurelio!" I said, smiling eagerly. "*Como esta, amigo?*" I still enjoyed testing my limited Spanish on him, a friendly gesture from the occasional speaker of one romance language to another, but as usual he wasn't obliging. The look he returned was one of tedium and ongoing contempt.

"*Mierda*," he said with his usual bluntness. "Not you."

"Swell location for a bar," I answered, ignoring the taunt. "Right across the street from AA."

"What you *want*, Eddie? And you *ain't* my *amigo*."

"Who says I want something?" I said, ambling over toward him. I kept up the shameless grin, but his scowl deepened.

"You're fulla shit, Eddie. You know that? One o' these days, you're gonna fuckin' explode right there on the street from all that shit you got stuffed inside you. You know what I mean? The biggest shit storm ever to hit Brooklyn. Take a whole fuckin' month to clean it up."

"What kind of talk is that?" I asked, taking the seat across from him. "I've always been a pal, haven't I? I went to your deathwatch, didn't I? At that charity hospital? Give me some credit."

"Sure, sure. You came lookin' so I could find out more shit for you before I croaked. Just like now. You want some shit about somebody, so you come to me again. Well, I don't got to do it this time, see? I don't got to do it anymore if I don't want to. I got enough problems."

"You telling me you've retired?"

"No. But I'm particular about who I work for these days. No damn *pendejos*, for sure. And I take cold, hard cash now. No J.T.S. Brown. Hard cash only. *Comprende?*"

"How much?"

"Depends on the job."

"I need to find out about some people who work for Jimmy Santini," I said.

"*Some* people?"

I already knew something about Santini's wife, his daughter, and his two sons, the Barracuda Brothers, so I limited myself. "I'm talking about his lawyer, his daughter's psychiatrist, and his chauffeur," I said. "I'll need physical descriptions, and as much background as you can get. What'll that cost me?"

He smiled at me for the first time. "Depends," he said again, and took a swig of his 7-Up, straight from the bottle.

"Go easy on that stuff," I said, scowling back at him.

"It's the new Aurelio, see? Ridin' high on the wagon these days. Everything in fuckin' moderation."

"I hope so," I said.

"You can fuckin' count on it."

I got up from the booth. "I'll be at the office for the next couple of hours. You can call me there. If you feel like it."

He shook his head.

"You're saying no?" I said.

"No phone calls. I don't do phone calls no more, neither. Be at Nero's at six o'clock tonight, and you'll get what I find, if I feel like findin' it. And if it ain't what you're lookin' for, that's too fuckin' bad."

"You're not getting more than a Ulysses S. Grant," I said, offering a cheapskate scowl. "No matter what you find."

"You're all heart," he said.

"That's what my wife tells me. Every once in a while when I'm not in the dog house."

"Smart lady," he said, and I walked out.

Arnie Pulaski, my junior partner, was waiting for me at the office, looking out the window at the rain and sleet that were still falling. He had his feet up on my desk, and the current copy of *Playboy* was in his lap, open to the centerfold. We'd been partners for about eight months now, partners for the second time, actually, but that's another story that isn't worth going into.

"Mornin', boss," he said, grinning.

"First, get out of my chair," I said, and he stood up. I tossed my damp fedora onto the hat rack, sat behind my desk, and glared at him. "I'm not sure why, but I guess I'm glad you're here," I said. "Now I won't have to go searching for you in all the dirty book stores."

"Not much goin' on," said Arnie with his customary nonchalance. "And the weather's just plain shitty."

"Well, there's something going on now," I said. "And I'm going to need everybody who works for me on double overtime."

"Everybody?"

"You, Liam, and anybody else we can get. I'm hoping that Watusi's available."

"Oh, Jesus, not the big spook."

"Yeah. And you'd better mind your manners with him. He can break you like a pretzel."

"If he don't bore me to death first with all those big words."

"Like I said, partner. Finesse him."

"So, what's the deal?" said Arnie, folding up Miss March and giving me his semi-best attention.

"Surveillance job. It's not exactly easy money, but there'll be plenty of it, if we do it right."

"Do *what* right, Eddie lad?" It was Liam O'Rourke, strolling into the office. I hadn't seen Liam in a while, but he looked unchanged. Rail thin, dark, sunken eyes, and stone deaf in one ear from a case back in '49. Enough serious character flaws for a dozen men, but he was still my favorite Irishman.

"You must be psychic," I said. "Anyway, I was just about to call you."

"Saved you the trouble, then."

"No limerick?" I asked. "To mark the occasion?" Reciting off-color poetry was one of Liam's more endearing peculiarities.

"If I knew what the occasion was, Eddie lad..."

So I sat them both down and explained.

"Sweet Jaysus," said Liam when he'd heard it all.

"We're tailin' *how many* people?" asked Arnie. "In shifts? That's fuckin' impossible." Liam was shaking his head in agreement.

"There's seven, all right," I said. "Could've been one more, but he's long gone." I was thinking of an underboss who had once worked for Santini, a guy named John Bologna, aka Johnny Baloney. Ambitious, intelligent, devious, and very deadly. Fortunately, he'd ridden the Sparky up at Sing Sing back in '56, and Santini had never replaced him.

"Jesus," said Arnie. "*Seven* fuckin' suspects?"

"Well, that's what we're doing," I said. "And nobody can know about it. We're going to be discreet, and we're going to be damn careful. Jimmy Santini's not your average client. The usual rules of engagement don't apply."

"There's still only three of us, lad," said Liam. "What about that little dee-tail?"

"Four, if I can get Watusi," I said. "I wish the situation was different, but it's not, and I don't have the option to back out of this job until Santini says so. If either of you wants to get out before things heat up, now's the time."

"I'm in," said Arnie.

"We're both in, Eddie lad."

"All right, then. Let's divide up the suspects. For starters, I'll take the Barracuda Brothers."

"Who?"

"Carmine and Rico, Jimmy Santini's idiot sons. I'll take them as a pair. They're just about inseparable. Do just about everything together. That means, assuming that I can get Watusi, we only need two more guys to run the minimal surveillance, such as it is. You know anybody?"

"I got an old buddy from the Marines," said Arnie. "If the pay's good, he'll want in. Silent as a ghost. Eyes like a hawk. Nerves of steel. Company sniper back in Korea. You can count on him."

"All right," I said. "Let me know if and when he's ready."

"He'll be ready."

"And Arnie, if your guy becomes a problem, he's *your* problem."

"Understood."

"Anybody want to keep tabs on the daughter?" I asked.

"I'll take her," said Arnie. "She lives at home, right?"

"Maria. Daddy's Little Girl," I said. "She'd be about thirty now."

"You know her?"

"Well enough. Be wary of her. I had some trouble that involved her back in '47."

"Well, I'll take still her," said Arnie.

"With *finesse*, partner. And keep your goddamn distance. You don't have to get her into bed, just keep tabs on her."

"Sure, sure."

"I can cover Santini's old lady," said Liam.

"Name's Wanda. And she's not all that old," I said. "His second wife, actually. The first died when the daughter was born. If she's married to Santini, she's nobody's fool, so don't underestimate her, and don't crowd her. In fact, don't crowd *any* of these people. If we screw up, or if any of them makes us, the game's over, in more ways than one."

"And the other three?" asked Arnie. "The lawyer, the shrink, and the chauffeur. Who's gonna cover them?"

"I've got Aurelio checking up on them. He'll get me physical descriptions and some background. Your buddy from the Corps can have one of them, and if I can get Watusi, he'll take another."

"That still leaves one more, lad," said Liam. "One uncovered."

"And don't I know it," I said.

"And they're all people that Santini suspects?"

"Every damn one."

"You're sure?"

"*He's* sure," I said, "and he's the one paying us. Seventeen hundred dollars apiece."

"And just *how* does he know?" asked Arnie. "Tell me again."

I smiled. "He said a little bird told him."

"Well, for one, I don't care if a gypsy fortune teller told the bloke," said Liam. "It's good money."

"When do we start?" asked Arnie.

"Right now."

"Now? I got a date."

"No you don't," I said. "Until further notice, you've got a job," and I walked out of the office.

5

My first choice to tail our final suspect was Frankie DeFilippo, my barber and best friend since grammar school. I'd always been reluctant to enlist the help of friends in my shamus pursuits. An overeager amateur can get himself killed, and you right along with him, but I didn't mind so much making the offer on surveillance cases: just follow somebody around, take notes on where he goes and when, who he meets, and then report back. And if somebody spots you doing it, run like you were in the Olympics. I had two other old friends -- Angelo Napolitano and Tony Mirabello -- who would have gladly volunteered for any job I offered, but they weren't the brightest bulbs, and I wasn't about to trust them with anything more serious than mailing a letter. Even if it were a cakewalk, the job wouldn't involve Angelo or Tony.

Frankie, who'd piloted a B-24 Liberator during the war, was more than able enough, and he was proficient with his fists; but Frankie wasn't at his barbershop, and there was a handwritten sign in the window that said: 'Gone Fishing.' Frankie didn't fish, but I could pretty well guess what the sign meant. Most of his sudden, unexplained absences from the tonsorial arts had to do with the latest pretty girl he'd discovered. Past forty, and still chasing the skirts like an oversexed teenager. Not finding Frankie at his shop, I decided to pay a visit to St. Margaret's Parochial, where we'd all gone to elementary school. Angelo was the janitor there, and my daughter Amanda was a student in the first grade. It was possible, even likely, that Frankie -- a shameless braggart as well as a lothario -- had made his amorous intentions known to Angelo before he'd left, so I went looking. I found Angelo in the building's dim basement fussing with the oil furnace.

"Darn," said Angelo, that being his strongest epithet. "Wish we still had the old coal furnace."

"Oh?"

"This thing breaks down all the time. Sure wish they hadn't gone all modern on me. It was a good furnace, too, that old coal furnace, and it worked swell."

I smiled, but the thought that brought it to mind was one I'd chosen a long time ago to keep to myself. I had killed a man in this very basement back in '47. Killed him right under Angelo's innocent nose and burned his body in the coal furnace. To keep Angelo from finding out what I'd done there, I'd even volunteered to clean out the ashes afterward. Angelo saw it as a favor I'd done him; but the bigger favor was not giving him the awful knowledge of what I'd done. Knowledge his simple mind could not handle. Even the fact that it was self-defense, and that the man had been waiting there to kill me, wouldn't have helped. The coal furnace was gone now, and the man's disappearance long forgotten, but the grim memory had stayed with me.

"Whatcha doin' here, Eddie?" It was Angelo's voice. I had been wool gathering. I smiled at him.

"Was in the neighborhood," I said. "Seen Frankie around?"

"Frankie?" he said, screwing up his face.

"DeFilippo. Do we know any other Frankies?"

"Oh. Don't know, Eddie," he said. "Ain't seen him."

"Since when?" I asked, and he noticed the burr in my voice.

"Geez, Eddie, I don't know. Just ain't seen him for a while. He let me go to the pictures with him coupla weeks ago: *Absent-Minded Professor.*"

"Did he have a girl?"

"Sure. He's always got a girl." He smiled as he tapped the glass on one of the meters with a screwdriver.

"Well, if you hear anything, let me know," I said. "I gotta talk to him about something important. Something that can't wait."

"Can *I* help ya, Eddie?" he asked.

"It's gotta be Frankie."

"Maybe he un-loped with somebody," Angelo said. "He sure likes the pretty girls."

"I doubt it," I answered on my way out. "And the word is 'e-loped.'"

"Oh," said Angelo, and made another tap on the meter glass.

"Catch you later," I said, and left him.

It occurred to me on my way back that I might have that little talk about beatniks with Gino's daughter Gloria before things heated up with Santini; but as far as I was concerned, it was her business with whom she spent her time, and not mine. Like so many doting fathers of teenage girls, Gino was hanging on when he should have been letting go. My three sisters had received the same treatment from our parents before they were married off to the three biggest jerks in Brooklyn, but that's also another story. When you're the oldest, and the only boy in the family, like me, your parents pretty much let you go your own way, to work things out on your own, even if that means going the *wrong* way for a while. My mother had told me once, and only once, never to do anything that I'd be ashamed to tell her about. And so I never did tell her.

I stopped off at Nero's early, hoping that Aurelio was there and that he had the information I'd asked him for, but the place was empty in mid-afternoon. As I sat at the bar, nursing a cold Schaefer, I considered my final choice for the surveillance team. His given name was Elijah Hamilton, but he had chosen to call himself Watusi after a tribe of fierce, monumental men from central Africa. He was the only friend I had who was black, and I was his only friend who wasn't. Until only last year, I was certain that I could count on him for just about anything; but we'd had a falling out over his daughter, Desiree, who'd fallen in love with a white man named Jerry. I'd defended her, Watusi had taken offense, and though we'd seemed to have patched things up, I still wasn't sure he would agree to work for me again. I already knew he didn't care much for surveillance jobs, especially in white neighborhoods. I tried, in vain, to remember the last time we'd spoken in friendship.

Laura was in the kitchen when I got home. Mary was in her bed napping, and Amanda wasn't due back from St. Margaret's until after three o'clock. I wasn't sure what kind of reception I would get from Laura after this morning's trouble, so I was wary.

"I got all the stuff you wanted from Gino's," I said from the kitchen doorway.

She half-smiled. "I can see that," she answered, and then the smile widened a little before fading again. It was that smile that had first drawn me to her back in '52, back when her younger brother Johnny had a gambling problem and not the best class of friends. That and the way her slim hips moved tantalizingly under her dress. She'd appeared out of the blue one lazy summer afternoon while I was drinking a glass of lemonade on my front stoop. Maybe it wasn't as romantic a first meeting as the one between Antony and Cleopatra or Napoleon and Josephine, but not bad, all things considered.

"Are you still angry?" I asked. "I mean, about having those 'guests' this morning?"

"Shouldn't I be?"

"Well, sure," I said, and waited for the other shoe to drop. In times past like these, times of perceived or real dangers, she'd sometimes gone to stay with her parents, the Temafontes, or packed the kids off to Detroit to stay with her brother, who had since given up the gambling habit. What she might do now, given her current mood, was anybody's guess. "As soon as the job's done, Laura, I swear it. As soon as it's done and Santini's satisfied..."

"*Will* he be satisfied?"

I sighed before I spoke. "I hope so."

"I'm counting on you to be careful, Eddie. Your children are, too."

"I know. I will be."

"I hope you're right about this. If you're wrong, and I'm a widow..."

"Laura..."

"And your children are fatherless..."

"I'll be careful," I said. "Anyway, it's only a surveillance."

"Only?"

"I promise."

"All right," she said, giving me a penetrating look. "And are you home for the rest of the day now? Will you be here for the girls tonight at bed time?"

I wanted to say yes, but I couldn't promise. There was nothing I wanted to do more than stay home with my wife and kids; but I still had the meeting with Aurelio at six, and there was one more thing before that: finding out if Elijah Hamilton, aka Watusi, and I were still friends.

6

Watusi lived in a modest garden apartment on West 131st Street, not far from Striver's Row. For a white man, driving there was safer than going to any of Watusi's previous addresses around 125th Street. My cars and I had been protected at one time in Harlem by a vice lord known as the King of Africa, but he'd been dead these many years, murdered by one of his many competitors. Just a ghost now from a long-abandoned past. There were other ghosts from that part of Harlem as well, including Alma, the mother of Watusi's only child, and the one great love of his life. Too many ghosts there, in those haunted old places, and so Watusi had found a new refuge and some occasional peace here in East Harlem -- Spanish Harlem.

He was an even more solitary man these days. His daughter Desiree and her white husband Jerry lived in Chicago now, where she was a promising ballerina and part-time instructor with the Joffrey Ballet. Old Mrs. Crosse, Watusi's long-time neighbor at his last address, had died in December. She'd been his last reason for staying there, and so he'd pulled up stakes and moved the mile or two away that put him now on West 131st Street. He was indeed a private man, and never an easy man to befriend. He'd recovered from the fact that his daughter had fallen in love with a white man against his wishes, married him, and was now expecting a mulatto child, but he was still opposed to a mingling of the races. Thanks to her, however, he had become more accepting of at least a few whites other than myself, and thanks to her, he had even been on semi-speaking terms with my sisters and their husbands for a while. But there had always been more forced civility than genuine warmth in their exchanges at family barbecues in once-forbidden Bensonhurst. Finally, without his daughter to coax him, he'd just stopped going there with me. The larger world hadn't changed much for him, either. Most whites were still his natural enemies, and there were times when I felt him ever so subtly slipping away from our long and oft-tested friendship.

This time, however, he smiled broadly as he opened the door. He led me through his Spartan rooms to the neat, trim garden behind them, where he offered me a glass and a cold bottle of Schaefer. He had a pair of red Adirondack chairs in the garden, and he wiped them scrupulously dry with a towel as I admired a bed of budding tulips along the back fence. The sleet of earlier in the day had changed to rain only about an hour before, and then the rain had stopped completely. The sun was out, finally, and it was almost warm.

"I received a letter from Desiree just yesterday," he announced with pride as he took the chair next to mine. "The baby is due in about a month, if it's on time. If it's a female child, they have promised to name it Alma, after Desiree's mother. If it's a male child, they'll name it Thomas after my adoptive father. Of course, she'll be on maternity leave from the Joffrey for a while, but she expects to be back on her toes, as it were, when rehearsals start for *The Nutcracker* in the fall."

"That's good news, Tooss. Send her my best."

I took a pull on my cold Schaefer and looked over at him in the other Adirondack chair. After almost losing his life on our last case a year ago, he looked remarkably like his old self: erudite, cultured, monumental. There must have been something disturbing in the look I offered him, because he stiffened and gave me an odd look back.

"Is it cold enough?" he asked. "The beverage?"

"Yes, it's fine."

"And how are things in lily-white Bensonhurst?"

"They're fine. Everything's fine."

"Are you sure?" he asked, his eyes boring in now.

"Of course," I said. "Why do you ask?"

"I can see that this is not a social visit, Eddie. Forgive my candor, but it is written all over your white face."

"I could use some help, yes," I said.

"Explain it to me, then."

When I finished, he nodded and said, "I see the reason for your discomfort now. And you are unable to say no to this man Santini?"

"That's right."

"A surveillance, you say."

"Yes."

"And you are two operatives short."

"Yes."

"So you've come to ask for my help."

"Yes."

"I'm pleased to provide it, as much as I can, but that still leaves you a man short, does it not?"

"Yes."

He stood up from his chair and began to pace restlessly in the yard. I stood up with him. Finally, he stood still and looked at me. The look was piercing, but still amicable. "I could provide that man for you, Eddie, but I'm not entirely sure you would want him."

"If he's somebody you'd vouch for, I'd ask no questions. Who is he? What's his name?"

"Aabidullah Bashir. It is a Muslim name. He is a follower of a man known as Malcolm X."

"And?"

"You would have known him by a different name. Viper Robinson."

I sat down as if I'd been pole axed. Viper Robinson was perhaps my greatest living enemy. He'd sworn to kill me back in '46 just before he'd killed a colored man who was an enemy of Watusi. He'd fled to the West Coast, hopefully without any thought of returning to New York; but his vengeful shadow had never left me, and I still feared him above all other men. Now he was apparently back in the city, and I could only believe that his feelings toward me hadn't changed.

"You're sure he's back?" I asked.

"I talked to him only yesterday. On the telephone."

"And he still wants me dead?"

"I did not ask, but..."

"I'm going to have enough trouble watching my back with Jimmy Santini," I said. "Fighting a war on two fronts is a lousy idea. Do you know anybody else?"

"Viper -- Aabidullah -- is in desperate need of money," argued Watusi. "That might be a mitigating factor, enough to put him off, assuming that he still wishes you harm, until the surveillance ends. After that, who can say what he'll do? Not I. He has always been somewhat mercurial."

"Somewhat? You were always good at understatement, Tooss," I said, making a face.

"Fifteen years is a long time, Eddie. The man you knew as Viper may have used that time to reconsider his life -- and yours. The fact that he has found religion is partly proof of that, of his ability to change. To forgive, if not quite to forget. Of course, I cannot promise that he will see you differently now, but I think you owe him the opportunity to show it if he can. If it did nothing else, it might solve your current employment problem."

"The answer still has to be 'no,' Tooss."

"What if I spoke to him about it? What if I could arrange a meeting with you here? The very fact that he *has* returned, with a murder charge still hovering over him, indicates that some part of him *has* changed. He's taking a very great risk to be here under any name. For something. For a reason that is important to him."

"That's part of what worries me," I said. "And he didn't tell you why he came back?"

"No."

"I really don't want to find out the hard way," I said.

"Let me try, then."

"All right," I said. "But I'll be carrying heat at that meeting, just the same."

I was due back home, but I had one more stop to make before I could read to my little girls at bedtime. Aurelio Rodriguez was just where he said he'd be at six that evening. He was nursing another bottle of 7-Up in his favorite corner booth at Nero's. He held out his hand, palm open, when I sat across from him.

"Have you got something?"

"Find out, *amigo*," he said.

"Are we friends again, then?"

"Maybe."

"How much?" I asked. He flashed ten fingers at me.

"I said fifty, not a hundred."

He stood up, smiling. "Okay. If you don't want the dirt from me anymore, I know this guy who works a little cheaper. His name is Enrico Rosario. He's a rummy, so he wouldn't be in my league, but he'll probably take less."

"Sit down, *amigo*," I said. "I guess you'll have to do." I handed him a pair of Ulysses S. Grants. He sat down.

"The lawyer's name is Fanucci. Giorgio Fanucci. Harvard Law. He's got an office over near Borough Hall. In his mid-forties, never married, balding, and on the skinny side. Wears three-piece Brooks Brothers suits, but they look cheap on him. Drives a Mercedes. Been Santini's mouthpiece for the last ten years. Never been in trouble with the law. Squeaky-clean. Has only one client, and that's your man Santini."

"Santini is his *only* client?"

"That's what I'm saying."

"And the psychiatrist?"

"Meyer Rothberg. NYU grad. Got a nice little castle on Albemarle Road. On the stocky side, but he keeps fit. Shows up almost every morning at that gym on New Utrecht."

"Costello's," I said.

"That's the place, *amigo*."

"Anything else on him?"

"Mid-thirties, also never married, but he plays the field like a stud horse. Lots of ladies, and all respectable."

"Okay. And what about the chauffeur?"

He frowned. "There's a problem there."

"Oh?"

"Other than his name, description, and address, I got nothing. A big zero."

"I'm paying you two General Grants for a big zero?" I said, my tone turning irritable.

"Hey, *amigo*, if you want the dirt on guys like Santini, my sources, they got no problem. But try to find anything on the average Joe, and they don't even know where to start. They only know the real bad guys and the high rollers, *comprende*? This chauffeur, he's got no record. Not even a misdemeanor. And he's a complete nobody. All I know is he's Harry Appolino, and he lives in an apartment above a delicatessen on Bay Parkway. In his late twenties, dark, average height, been in Santini's employ for about three months. No points against him on his license. You wanted me to find out for you, and that's what I found out."

"Anything else?"

"That's it, unless you want me to check out somebody else. But that'll be another hundred."

"That's enough for now," I said, and stood up.

"Hey, where you going, *amigo*? The night is young."

"Home," I said, "where my kids are waiting to be read to, and where my wife is probably waiting with a loaded shotgun."

"All the more reason to stay away."

"Got to face her sometime."

"Put it off for a while. Have a 7-Up with me. Come on, *amigo*. We'll see if we can get drunk on the stuff."

"Since when are you looking for us to be pals?" I asked. "Most of the time, you can't wait to get rid of me."

"And vice-versa, man."

"I'm tired," I said. "Don't you ever get tired?"

"Maybe I'm lonely," he said, flashing a caustic grin. "I don't got the bottle to keep me warm anymore. I don't got nothin' to keep me warm anymore. *Comprende*?"

"Another time, maybe."

"There may not *be* another time, *amigo*," he said, giving me a sideways look.

"There's truth in that," I said. "Yessir. Plenty of truth in that."

"Come on, *amigo*. Stick around. Be my pal just this one time. Drink a fuckin' 7-Up with me."

"No time," I said. "Honest."

"You're gonna be sorry you didn't stay."

"Okay, then, I'll be sorry."

"Always figured you for a killjoy," he said, handing me a manila envelope. "It's all in there. What I found. In case your dago memory fails you."

"I can't afford to fail at anything else," I said, and I left him alone in the dark.

7

Laura had the kitchen table set for one when I walked in. My two little girls were causing a commotion in their bedroom down the hall. Laura was still frowning.

"Amanda, Mary," I called out. "Daddy's home." I stole a look at Laura, then turned away before her own look turned me to stone. Like Viper Robinson, she had a long memory, and I was sure she'd been sharpening her claws, if not her knives, ever since this morning.

The girls raced out and into my arms. "Story time!" shouted Amanda. I'd been reading *The Wind in the Willows* to them. Mr. Toad of Toad Hall had just traded in his gypsy wagon for a fancy new motorcar, and all hell was breaking loose along the riverbank.

"Not tonight," said their mother sternly. "It's late, and Amanda, you have school tomorrow."

"Oh, mother!"

"No arguments. It's after seven. Now, get ready for bed."

"I'll read you a chapter," I said, staring boldly into the Medusa's eyes. "But only a short one. Mind your mother."

The girls moped back to their bedroom, and Laura gave me the punishing look again.

"Are we going to fight?" I asked. "I really don't want to. After this morning, my day only got worse."

"Oh?" she said, turning to the kitchen counter where she had dishes drying. "And what are you going to do about it?"

"*Do* about it?"

"Yes."

"It's kind of complicated," I said.

She turned to face me again, glaring. "So there's something else? Something more than having a pair of hoodlums invade our home? Something more than working for a Mafia boss? By all means, Eddie, *tell me* about it." Her voice was almost calm, but she had a tight, two-fisted grip on her apron that spoke volumes to me.

"So, you're not over it," I said haltingly.

"No, I'm not."

I paused for a moment to collect myself, to find the right words, if there were any. "There's no danger if I take on the work, Laura," I said finally. "There *is* danger if I don't."

"And you've *already* taken on the work, haven't you? That's what you *said*, isn't it?"

"Yes."

"Despite what happened here this morning. Despite that."

"I'm doing this because I *have* to, Laura," I said, my voice rising.

"And you're not going to the police?"

"No, I'm not."

"Your family has been threatened by mobsters, and you're *not* going to the police?"

"No. And nobody's threatened you."

"Fine. If you won't call the police, then I will." She brushed past me, toward the hall telephone. I stopped her.

"Laura, please listen to me. This is a standard surveillance job. Nothing more. I report to my client on what I find, and he does what he wants with the information. That's all there is to it. My client, Mr. Santini, is afraid for his life. He wants to know who in his closest circle wants to kill him. My job is to find out who that is if I can. And to prevent a murder."

"Then why were those men here?"

I didn't want to answer that.

"Why were they here, Eddie?"

"Did they threaten you?"

"No."

"Did they threaten the girls?"

"No, but..."

"Did they do anything to frighten you, anything at all, except to sit at your kitchen table without asking you first?"

"No."

"Laura, they were here so you wouldn't worry when I didn't come straight back from the grocery store. That's why they were here. And they *told* you so, didn't they?"

She didn't answer, so I backed off. I couldn't tell her what might have happened to any or all of us if I'd turned down Santini's offer, but I *hadn't* turned him down, so there was no point going into the details. It wasn't a lie exactly, not telling her, just a cautious omission. An omission that, hopefully, would keep her, the girls, all of us, out of harm's way.

"I still don't understand why he had to call *you*," she said. "Why *you*?"

"Because he trusts me."

"Why?"

"Because of something that happened a long time ago, before I knew you. I told him the truth about something when he knew I didn't have to. I helped him out, that's all, and he's trusted me ever since. Even though our paths haven't crossed in all that time. I think he's really afraid for his life, Laura. He can't trust any of the people around him -- that's what he thinks now, anyway -- so he's calling on me."

"Why wouldn't he call the police if he was in danger?"

"Because he *couldn't*. Don't you see? Any more than I could've asked Herman Goering to light my celebration cigar on V-E Day. The police won't be interested in helping Santini. They'll be trying to *get* him. They'll be hoping that the assassin *succeeds*."

"All right."

"So, we'll go about our business as usual. It's like any other case, but it's not something we talk to the neighbors about. And if we do things right, Santini will have his traitor, his would-be assassin, and that'll be the end of it as far as I'm concerned. As far as any of us is concerned. Okay?"

I saw the tension quietly slip out of her, and a small, fragile smile formed on her lips. "You'd better go in there now," she said, nodding in the direction of the girls' bedroom. "They're waiting for their story, and all hell will break loose if you're not there to read it to them."

"Sometimes I think I'm more afraid of crossing those two than I am of Santini," I said.

"Keep that thought in mind," she said, "and remember that I'll be right behind them."

In the morning, I went to the office early. The weather was more like real mid-April weather, and the skies were clear. I bought my copy of the *Daily News* from the newsstand, brewed myself a pot of A&P Bokar on the office hotplate, and waited for my operatives to arrive. Only then could the operation begin.

Arnie Pulaski was first, full of vinegar as always. "I talked to that Marine buddy of mine," he said. "Charlie Holloway. He'll cover the chauffeur for you."

"There's not a whole lot of information on the chauffeur from my usual sources," I explained. "I'd make him our most minor suspect at this point. Your buddy might not have a lot to do, but at least he won't have to watch his back."

"He'll be happy enough," said Arnie. "As long as he collects his pay."

"He'll get it if he tends to his work. Now, about Santini's daughter. Remember what I told you. Finesse. Lots of finesse. Keep sharp, and always keep your distance. Just tell me where the princess goes, what she does, and who she sees."

"I already did some checking on the little lady. She drives a pink T-Bird. Can you believe it? Pink! It'll be a piece of cake followin' her. And she ain't bad to look at, either."

"The lady was going to be a nun once. Did you know that?"

"A nun?" He laughed.

"A long time ago."

"Doesn't that kind of leave her off your killer list? Almost bein' a nun and all?"

I grinned. "You ever go to Catholic school?"

He shook his head. "P.S. 128."

"You don't know much about nuns, then. And anyway, being a nun wasn't her idea. Far from it."

He smiled, then paused in the doorway. "Wanna tell me one more time why this Santini hood thinks somebody wants to kill him?"

"He didn't tell me," I said.

"But he's sure? And he's got *seven* suspects?"

"That's what he said. You got a bug up your ass, Arnie?"

"No, but..."

"But what?"

"*Seven*? Seven people? You ever give any thought that this guy is maybe just crazy? I mean, like some special kind of crazy? Whatta you call it when somebody thinks everybody's after him, but nobody is? He's... what's the word?"

"Paranoid?"

"Yeah, that's it. You think maybe he's just paranoid, and there's nobody at all who wants to kill him?"

"Given his chosen line of work, and the possibility that he might have a nagging conscience hidden away deep somewhere, it wouldn't surprise me either way," I said. "And if that's how it plays out, we just do our job, tell him the good news when we're done, and take our well-earned money. Are you okay with that?"

"You bet, partner," he said.

I sent him on his way just as Liam arrived. Liam, true to form, went straight for the coffee pot.

"You got a plan for today?" I asked.

"Keepin' tabs on the lady of the house, I'm expectin'."

"If she takes her own car, you follow her, but back off if the chauffeur drives her. I've already got a man on him. No sense in crowding the field. If she does take her own car, it's the not-so-usual places she goes that'll interest me most. Still, keep track of everything. Places, times, length of stay, etcetera. Okay? And let's not all bunch up our cars outside the gates at Santini's. Just park somewhere close enough to see who goes in and out of those gates."

"You can count on me, lad. And your own two, the brothers? What about them?"

"I've been giving them some extra thought. I just can't picture them at odds with Santini, with their father. They've always idolized him; but then it's been a while. The atmosphere might have changed. It's an odd family, in any case."

"That it is, lad. And the other two suspects?"

"That's the other problem. I can put Watusi on one of them, but I'm not sure about the second. Watusi offered a guy, a colored guy, to do the work, but this particular colored guy has had it in for me for a long time. I don't think I can trust turning my back on him."

"Rock and a hard place, lad."

"Make that seven rocks," I said.

At the end of the day, I returned to the office. I'd hoped to get some leads by following the Barracuda Brothers, but there were none. The Brothers had gone nowhere all day. Usually, they made the rounds of friendly drinking holes, pool halls, gambling rooms, dirty bookshops, and strip clubs, their favorite of the latter being the Pom Pom Club in Borough Park. I still had mixed feelings about that place. My first carnal experiences with a real live woman had happened there when I was in my teens; but the exotic dancer there named Betty Barbera who'd taught me those skills had been murdered in '47, the same case in which I'd killed the hood in the basement of St. Margaret's and burned him up in the coal furnace.

The news from my three operatives hadn't been much better. The pink T-Bird had gone nowhere, and Mrs. Santini was also staying put. Arnie and Liam reported back frowning and shaking their heads, and Arnie brought his Marine buddy's empty report on the chauffeur and the limousine. Watusi as yet had no one to follow, and there was no way I figured that Viper would work out, meaning that one of the seven suspects would get no coverage at all. Suddenly, the surveillance began to look ridiculous in the extreme. What were we doing, following these people? Who said that any of the suspects, aside from the lawyer and the shrink, had to be away from the grounds to kill Santini? Given the easy possibility of one or all of them snuffing him right at home, what was the point in tailing anybody anywhere? More importantly, maybe Arnie was right. Maybe this whole phony drama had originated in the unsound mind of an aging mobster, a man with a world of enemies, a man suddenly afraid of everybody and everything.

"Well," said Arnie, lounging in the stuffed armchair I kept for my clients, "This could be a big waste of time. How long is he givin' us to find this assassin, anyway?"

"It's open-ended," I said.

"No shit?"

"No shit."

"So we keep tailin' these people until hell freezes over?"

"Something like that, Arnie."

"A fookin' poor arrangement, if you're askin' me," said Liam.

I gave them a hard look. "You both had your chance to opt out. You can still do it, but I won't take it kindly, and you won't work for Lombardi Investigations any more, either of you."

"And the big spook, and his... friend?" said Arnie.

"Watusi, yes, probably. The other one, no."

"Back tomorrow, then?" said Liam.

"If you still want a job," I said, and they left.

I sat in my office chair for a long time, swiveling every once in a while to hear the familiar squeak that it made. I was going to call Watusi and tell him that Viper would be unacceptable, that I could never work with him. Then the phone rang.

It was Watusi. Viper Robinson wanted to talk, he said.

Right now.

8

Viper wanted to meet on neutral ground, Watusi explained, a fried chicken place in Stuyvesant called Talley's Fried Chicken. I'd been there only once before, back in '48 during a case that involved a shape-shifting psychopath named Jack Janus and Watusi's adoptive father, Thomas Hamilton. It wasn't a place that I was eager to return to for any number of reasons, but Watusi gave me the usual assurances, and so I agreed to the meeting. All that notwithstanding, before I went to pick him up, I slipped my .38 revolver into the red leather holster under the right arm of my suit jacket before I left the office.

I called Laura to tell her that I wouldn't be home for dinner and drove first to Watusi's place in Spanish Harlem and then to Talley's. Watusi was noticeably silent during the drive, and I'd already decided to keep my thoughts to myself. After we'd parked on Fulton Avenue, he spoke for the first time.

"Is that bulge under your jacket what I imagine it is?" he asked in a warning tone.

"It is," I said.

"Not the best way to begin a meeting."

"It's the only way I'm going in there, Tooss," I said, and we walked into Talley's.

I remembered the familiar smells first -- chicken fat, cigarette smoke, waves of perspiration -- but I'd forgotten about the noise. Places like Talley's were always busy this time of day, but the constricted space and the low ceiling intensified every conversation in the room and every sound from the kitchen. Watusi, standing just in front of me, blocked the view, and I waited for a moment in his great shadow as he surveyed the place. When he moved, I moved, but I couldn't see where we were going except deeper into Talley's, deeper into a hostile territory, into a place of danger and uncertainty. I saw the faces of colored men as we maneuvered through the long, narrow room, and those men looked back at me. The looks were feral, hostile, suspicious. Wherever a woman, or a child and a woman, sat with a man, the looks were less challenging; but there were no welcoming faces in Talley's, or anywhere else where these people lived, for a man with white skin.

Watusi appeared to have reached the deepest extremity of Talley's when he opened a green metal door and we found ourselves in a part of the place that was almost silent. A faded wooden sign above the door just ahead said: TOILET. A doorway just to the right opened into a small office. There was a table there, and two folding chairs. Viper Robinson was sitting in one of them, under a light bulb with a flimsy green plastic shade over it.

"Glad you could come, brother. Have a seat," he said, looking at Watusi. The tone was as polite as the words, but then he saw me. "Should I get another chair for your white friend?" he asked. Before Watusi could give him an answer, I gave him my own.

"I'll stand," I said.

We glared at each other, examined each other like hungry animals eyeing prey. He was thinner than I'd remembered him, and he wore a graying goatee now to cover a somewhat underdeveloped chin. There was a scar under that goatee, and we both knew who'd put it there almost fifteen years ago. He wore glasses now, with wire rims. No hat. All of his clothing was black. It was both an identity and a warning.

"It's been a long time, White Boy," he said through a thin smile.

"I still have a name," I said.

"You always did," he answered, and his smile curved downward into a frown. "Never did like it much, though."

"Let me make this meeting short," I said. "I don't need any help at the moment. Especially yours."

"Don't you? That's not what I'm hearing."

"You're hearing it from me. Here and now."

He grinned again. "You think I'm going to snuff the man I'm working for, the man who's going to pay me wages, even if he is a cracker?"

"That would take some forbearance on your part. Forbearance is an attribute you've never had."

"*Forbearance. Attribute.* Well, now. You still studying vocabulary?"

I turned and started for the door.

"*Don't you turn your back on me, White Boy!*" he shouted, loud enough for Talley's clientele to hear him. I turned back.

"Still a bit touchy, aren't you, Viper?"

"My name is Aabidullah."

"Not to me," I said. "And my name isn't White Boy."

"Can we call a truce for a moment?" It was Watusi's voice, calm but urgent. "You two gentlemen have some need of each other, do you not?"

"There seems to be some debate on that point, Tooss," I said.

Viper didn't speak, but his look changed slightly. Calmer and less confrontational. I decided to match it, if only for Watusi's sake.

"We need to update some personal history," said Watusi in his most scholarly voice, as if we were his students and this small, dark office was a classroom, or at least a place of learning. "Aabidullah, who you once knew as Viper Robinson, is a family man now, Eddie. Two young boys. He's here in New York because of some trouble in Los Angeles that he didn't cause, but for which he has been blamed. He can't go back, and he cannot send for his family until he has the funds to do so. He can't just look anywhere in this city for work, as you well know. If you hire him for this job, he will be able to send for his family and go somewhere where he -- and they -- can be, finally, left alone."

"Is he wanted by the cops in L.A.?" I asked.

"You can talk to me, cracker," said Viper, still barely holding back his anger. "I'm sitting right here."

"Well, *are* you wanted?" I asked.

"You ever been to L.A.?" he asked, almost pleasantly. I had, back in '55, as part of that duck case out on the Island, but it was easier to lie about it. Even Watusi hadn't been around for that one.

"No," I said. "Never been."

"Of course, you're white. Be different for you, wouldn't it?"

"Speak plainly," I said, scowling. "I'm short on time."

"Yeah, I'm wanted. Not for anything I did, but for what I *am*."

"You'll have to explain that," I said.

"The L.A. cops, they're no different from what you got here. If you're a man of color, that is. I've been clean, White Boy, *squeaky* clean, ever since I hauled my poor black ass out there to the Coast, my black tail between my legs. 'Yassah, mistah bossman, yassah.' That's what they expect you to say whenever they roust you on the street in the middle of the day for no damn reason. That's how a *good* nigger behaves, see? And that's how I gotta answer 'em if I don't want my skull cracked open by no billy club or have my ass thrown in jail. Well, I won't get on my *knees* to no cops. I won't be a good nigger. That's why they want me, why they got it in for me, and that's the truth. You ever heard of Malcolm X?"

"Not really."

"Well, Malcolm X, he says I don't have to put up with that shit. He says that I'm a man, as good as any white man, and I ought to be *treated* like a man. Are you understanding me yet?"

"Maybe," I said. I turned back to Watusi.

"Aabidullah, there are a few things you should know about Eddie also," continued Watusi, as if he hadn't been interrupted. "He's a family man as well now. Two fine daughters who love him and depend on him. And a wife that any man, black or white, would be fortunate to call his own. You are both different men than you were, and there are wounds that are waiting to be healed. You both need to understand that."

"All right," I said, looking hard at Viper. "Just for the moment, let's say I might be able to use you for this job. You're still wanted for first-degree murder in this state. The job means that you'll be watching a building or an office somewhere, possibly at night, and in a white neighborhood. Watusi's already had some trouble with cops doing stakeouts in white-only areas, but there aren't any arrest warrants out on him. Are you prepared for the possibility that you'll be found out?" I eyeballed him for a moment when he didn't answer, and then I waited.

"I got new papers," he said finally. "I had my name changed. It's all legal."

"And I'm telling you that it's still possible for the cops to find you out," I said. "Are you willing to take the chance?"

"I'm willing," he said.

"And after the job's finished?"

"You won't see my black ass any more."

"All right. You'll need a car. Do you have one?"

"I can get one."

"*Legally?*"

He stopped himself before answering. I thought for a moment that the invective Watusi had hoped to dispel might be returning.

"Friend of mine's car," he said, almost politely.

"All right, then. You'll be tailing a lawyer. His name is Giorgio Fanucci. He works for a mobster named Jimmy Santini. He's got an office in a two-story building near Borough Hall. He's on the second floor. His sign's out front, and there's a stairway that goes up to his office. It's the only office on that floor. That's the only place where you'll be able to watch him from, or tail him from. He lives in Brooklyn Heights, so you're not going anywhere near there, day or night. That creates a blind spot for us, especially if he's the guy we're looking for, but we'll have to live with that. Santini is paying us ten grand to do the job. Split six ways, that's about seventeen hundred apiece, payable on completing the work. The job is open-ended. We'll be at this job until we satisfy Santini one way or the other. Are you agreeable?"

"I'll need some money up front," he said. He didn't look daggers at me, and he didn't say 'White Boy.'

"How much will you need?"

"A hundred will do."

"All right. I'll get it to Watusi for you in the morning. And it's not a gift. Just an advance on the seventeen hundred. Agreed?"

"Agreed."

"The guy you're tailing, he's in his forties, thin, balding, dresses nice but looks unkempt in even the best suits. He drives a Mercedes. I want to know where he goes in the daylight hours, and who goes to see him. Can you get access to a camera? If not, I can get you one."

"I have a .35 millimeter, a Nikon. Telephoto lens," Watusi said.

"Okay, fine. Take pictures of everybody who goes in. Santini is his only client, so everybody who goes inside that office is going to be important."

"All right," he said.

"And myself?" asked Watusi. "Whom will I be shadowing?"

"Santini's daughter's psychiatrist. I'll give you the details on the way back to Harlem."

"Very well."

"It's done, then," I said, giving him a casual look. "You'll be reporting to Watusi." I turned as if to leave, but Watusi stopped me.

"Aren't we forgetting something?" he asked with an ever-enlarging grin. "When two men make a contract, an *oral* contract, there must be a handshake to seal the bargain. Well?"

Surprisingly, Viper stood up from his chair and, without delay, offered his hand. I was the one who hesitated, but finally, I took the few steps toward him, and we shook on it. Black on white. Flesh on flesh. It was a strange feeling, an impossible feeling, but it was happening.

"You gentlemen care to have dinner now?" Watusi asked. "Talley's is well-known for its fried chicken."

Neither Viper nor I responded, Watusi and I went out to my Chrysler, which had not been trashed, and we drove away. He was silent for most of the return trip, but when I parked outside his apartment, he had some parting words.

"Aabidullah will not disappoint you, Eddie. He needs this chance. For himself, and for his family. I will not lecture you this once on the black experience in America, but it is what has made Aabidullah, and before that the man you knew as Viper, the angry, desperate man he is. If you can see him, just this once, as a man without color -- *any* color -- you may begin to understand why he needs this chance. The odds have been stacked against him succeeding at anything for a long time. The white system that represses him..."

I smiled. "I thought I wasn't going to get a lecture," I said.

"Ah. *Mea culpa.*"

"That's Latin," I said. "And who the hell is this Malcolm X, anyway?"

"Someone from the future," he said, smiling, and then left me without another word.

Laura was waiting for me when I got home. She was sitting on the couch in the living room. She had a worried expression on her face, which was better than anger.

"You look tired," she said. "Did you eat?"

I shook my head and sagged down next to her.

"I can fix you something," she said. "A sandwich?"

"Okay. Are the girls asleep?"

"They missed their chapter from *Wind in the Willows.* They missed their father. They weren't happy about that."

"I'm working on it," I said.

"And I miss my husband. This business with the mobster -- how long will it take?"

"I don't know, Laura. Forever, maybe."

"That's too long."

"One damn day of it is too long."

"Are you having second thoughts, then?"

"For the third time," I said, and smiled.

9

The first full week of the stakeout did not go well. It was raining again, and the street outside Santini's gated estate had become a small lake. Santini himself never left the grounds, and the chauffeur only took Santini's wife to the beauty parlor on Ocean Avenue and back. The Barracuda Brothers, Carmine and Rico, spent their days shooting pool up at Ames in Manhattan and having extended lunches at places like Jack Dempsey's on 33rd Street and Randazzo's Clam Bar at Coney Island. Santini's daughter, Maria, took the pink T-Bird out twice to have lunch at Sardi's with some of her girlfriends and to buy a few trinkets from Bloomingdale's and Tiffany's. The lawyer that Aabidullah was covering went to his office every day, had a quick lunch at the Bickford's near Borough Hall, and then drove home to Brooklyn Heights at five o'clock sharp. Nobody visited his office except the postman. Santini's daughter's psychiatrist, Watusi's assignment, played golf in Dyker Heights on better days, got in his regular exercise at Costello's Gym, and watched the mudders race at Belmont Park when the rain persisted. Otherwise, he had steady business through the week. Fifty-minute hours, as they were called.

There was something else about the case that didn't bode well. Santini had promised to call often to check on my progress, but he hadn't called. Not once. And what could I tell him if he had? We could only cover Santini's seven suspects for part of a day, and even if we did it seven days a week, which we were already doing, one or more of our quarries could rob the Williamsburg Savings Bank at high noon and we wouldn't know about it until we read it in the newspaper. So I decided to make some changes. Watusi and I would shift to a night schedule, despite his objections, and I gave the other operatives some discretion in setting their own hours, based on the habits of our suspects. We'd still be deaf, dumb, and blind for more than half the time on any given day, but there seemed to be no other viable choices.

None at all.

That wasn't the only source of discouragement. The more I thought about it, the more Santini's plan began to look as if it were designed to fail. I began to think that this was just some bizarre and pointless game that he was playing with us. An expensive lark that he seemed more than happy enough to pay for. A trip down Alice's rabbit hole or into Mr. Badger's house, just for laughs. Ten thousand dollars was a lot of money to spend on a lark, a private joke, but Santini was spending it without complaint and without comment.

Why?

I decided to find out. I let the Barracuda Brothers go where they might for the next few hours and called Santini at home. He hadn't given me a private number, so I called the one listed in the telephone directory. A woman answered.

"Yes?" she said. Her manner was cold, harsh, and angry. The accent was mostly Brooklyn, but there was also some Long Island in it.

"Is this the Santini residence?" I asked politely.

"It is."

"May I speak with Mr. Santini, please?"

"Who the hell's calling?"

"I'm afraid I can't say."

"Well, whoever the hell you are, you're talkin' to his neglected wife, and the rat bastard's not here."

"Do you know where he might be?" I asked. "It's kind of important."

"I don't know, and I don't care. Whatta you think about that? Anyway, he'll be away for the whole weekend. He packed a bag, the sonofabitch."

"And you don't know...?"

"No, I *don't* know," she said, and slammed down the receiver.

The sound reverberated in my ears for a moment, a monumental echo bouncing off a large expanse of nothing. I looked out the window of my office and watched the steady rain splash and puddle on 18th Avenue until it began to hypnotize me. When I returned to my senses, it was still raining, but I had snagged an idea of sorts from out of the void and decided to act on it. I gassed up the Chrysler wagon at the corner Texaco and started the long, wet drive toward Wantaugh and the Jones Beach Hotel. There I expected to have a showdown with a certain mobster named James Santini. And why would I expect to find him there? Let's say a little bird told me.

There was an accident on the Shore Parkway, so I waited in the backed-up traffic in the steady rain until the road was clear again. Head-on collision. Sudden death on the highway. Somebody had been in the wrong lane, at the wrong time, traveling in the wrong direction. Like me. Like this whole crazy business. It was time to re-direct the traffic that I could control, turn everything back around so it made sense again. At least to me. And Santini, like it or not, was going to make it happen.

The parking lot at the Jones Beach Hotel was almost empty. There were only three cars. The one parked nearest the building, an aging Buick, probably belonged to the desk clerk. The second, parked haphazardly in two spaces, was a new Ford Fairlane. The third was a nondescript newer-model Chevy, the kind that Santini was likely to use when he needed anonymity. I glanced at the window of that room on the third floor where we'd met just a week ago. The blackout shade was drawn. He was in there, all right. I ignored the desk clerk, breezed through the lobby, took the stairs in a series of quick leaps, and positioned myself in front of the door. I listened for a moment and then knocked hard. I heard rustling sounds from inside. Sudden movement, but no voices. I knocked again, louder, and made my presence known in as rude a manner as I could manage.

"Santini! I have to talk to you!" I shouted through the door. "Right now!" I'd left off the *Mister* part on purpose.

"Who's that? Who's there?" was the quick response.

"Eddie Lombardi. Are you going to open the door, or are we going to talk through it? Your choice. And get rid of the bimbo."

Another silence, more rustling, and whispering.

"Okay, okay," was the almost panicked response. "Go back to your car and wait there. When you see me at the window, then come ahead."

"All right," I said.

"You wait there, see? Until I roll up the shade and you see me in the window. You got that?"

I didn't answer. I just walked back to the car. I was Alice again, waiting for my appointment with the Mad Hatter. That would happen, of course, only after his sex toy of the moment had fled the field. He wouldn't be happy about that, but I didn't care.

It took her only a few minutes to appear at the hotel entrance, headed for her car in the pouring rain. She was a peroxide blonde, in her mid-twenties, not as stacked as I might have expected, but then she was wearing a bulky raincoat. She drove away, and I waited for Santini to raise the window shade and welcome me in. It was another few minutes before he did that, and I went inside.

The door to the room was open, and Santini was seated in the same chair as last time, pretending to read the newspaper. The bed had been hastily made. Just like the woman in the parking lot.

"What the hell are you doin' here, Lombardi?" he said with a scowl. "I didn't call for you."

"Which is the very reason why I'm here, Jimmy," I said. "Was she a good lay?"

"What?"

"The bimbo. Was she good in bed?"

"What the hell are you talkin' about?"

I grinned at him boldly, fearlessly. "Never mind," I said. "By the way, you're reading your newspaper upside-down. I knew a guy in the 101st Airborne who could read a newspaper in a mirror, but I never knew anybody who could read one upside-down. What's your secret?"

"I asked what you're *doin'* here, shamus," he said, his voice stern, but also oddly hollow, like a voice in retreat. He pushed the newspaper aside.

"I told you -- *Jimmy*. You didn't call. You said you would. You said you expected progress. You wanted your money's worth. But you didn't call. Don't you even want to know what's going on? Or do you already know, because that's how you've set it up?"

"What the hell are you talkin' about?"

"The fact that you didn't call, and a few other things."

"Of course I called," he said, struggling to get the words out. "I called a whole bunch of times. Ain't my fault if you weren't in your office."

"I've got an answering service, *Jimmy*. Twenty-four hours a day, seven days a week. If you'd called my office and I didn't pick up, the service would have. So you're full of shit on that one...*Jimmy*."

"Okay, so I've been busy."

"Maybe your dick's been busy, but that's about all," I said.

He was out of the chair. *"What did you say?"* It was the oddest feeling, but *he* was the one who looked afraid now -- of me. So I kept up the attack.

"If this is some kind of stupid game we've been playing, I'm *done* playing. Do you *understand*? This murder plot, this impossible scenario, you cooked it up yourself, didn't you? Well, it's not funny. It never was, and unless you give me something I can use, the joke's over. You can keep your funny money, and you can go straight to hell. And one more thing. If anything bad ever happens to any of my family, or any of my friends, or any of the people I've put to work on this little pipe dream of yours, I'll fucking kill you myself."

We stood there for a moment, Santini rigid as a war memorial, but getting his color back, me quivering with rage, staring at each other. Finally, he offered a conciliatory smile and sat down.

"You've got a temper. I didn't remember you havin' one. That's good. I like a man who's got a temper. I also like a man who's got some fire in his *testicoli*. Sit down, Lombardi. Sit down and take a load off."

"If you don't mind, I'd like to stand and stay on the subject," I said, cooling a bit.

"Sit," he said. *"Per favore."*

I sat.

"First of all, I wasn't bullshittin' you about somebody wantin' to kill me. You think I was?"

"Something along those lines," I said.

"Well, there *is* somebody. Somebody close. I can't tell you how I know. I don't even *know* how I know. But I still *know*. Okay? Believe it. So, aside from me not callin' you every five minutes, what's your beef?"

"This surveillance thing won't work. I can't keep my operatives on it forever, and that's how long it'll take to come up with anything, if there *is* anything. They won't do it anymore, and neither will I. Not even for ten grand."

"And so you want -- what? More money?"

"I want out, that's what I want. I'll pay my operatives out of the five thousand you've already given me, and you can keep the rest. If you want protection, you've got what -- thirty or more soldiers?"

"I can't trust a one of 'em."

"Well, then it looks like somebody's really going to kill you, Jimmy, and that's a fact."

He mused for a moment in his chair, or pretended to. "You know, you're a big disappointment to me, Lombardi. Big disappointment. I expected more."

"So did I."

"Okay, okay. You've let me down. But I'm not gonna take it personal. I'm even gonna be generous this time. I'm gonna give you one more chance to make good."

"I don't think you understand..."

"Hear me out. Give it one more week. That's all. I got a feeling that whatever it is, it's close. Real close. Just one more week. Maybe somethin' will happen. If it doesn't, okay. The deal will be off, and you won't have to do this no more. Is that enough to make you happy?"

"All right," I said. "But..."

"You gotta have a little more faith in me, Lombardi. I ain't jokin' about this. Me gettin' killed, that ain't no joke, either. Okay?"

"All right," I said. "And the money's the same?"

"Ten grand, half of which you've already got, correct?"

"Yes."

"Okay, then. One more week. Seven little days," he said, smiling. And then he winked at me.

"Excuse me?" I said, and he winked again.

10

Arnie Pulaski and Liam were in the office when I got back. They wore the same matching looks of fatigue and frustration. I thought I might just tell them about my talk with Santini, but then I decided against it. I'd let them know when the time was right, and now didn't seem like the time.

"Well?" I asked them. "Anything to report?"

Liam groaned. "If the bugger's dear wife is out to ice him, why does she have to bore me to death first?"

"Beauty parlor again?" I asked.

"And lunch dates. And clothes shoppin'. And *more* shoppin'."

"Took her own car, did she?" I asked.

"The fookin' chauffeur didn't drive her, if that's what you mean. Waste o' time followin' her, if you ask me."

"Nobody's asking you," I said, and gave him a hard look.

"No lie," Arnie chimed in. "This whole business is a waste o' time. It's nuts."

"You get to follow an attractive woman around for a week and you're unhappy?" I said, scowling at him.

"Yeah, well, this chick is *weird*. Any time she drives the T-Bird, she's gotta put on a pair of prissy white gloves. That's all she uses 'em for –- drivin' the fuckin' T-Bird. It's seriously nuts."

"She may not be the only nut," I said.

"They're all a little 'round the bend if you ask me," said Liam. "And I know you're not askin'. So if you say we keep at it, then I guess we do."

"For the moment," I said. "Things might be changing."

"They'd better, lad."

I was on time for dinner that night. There was even time to read the girls another chapter of *The Wind in the Willows* before we tucked them into their beds. Laura and I sat close together on the

68

couch in front of the fireplace. The room smelled of sweet cedar and Laura's perfume. I felt relaxed for the first time in a week.

"I went to see him today," I said.

"The marriage counselor?" she said, and grinned. "Or maybe Father Giacomo?"

"Santini," I said, frowning back.

"Did it go well?"

"I think so. He's agreed to put a limit on the surveillance. One more week."

"And then?"

"Then it's over. One way or the other."

"Do you think he means it?"

"I'd like to."

"And he really believes that someone wants to kill him?"

"That's what he says."

"Do *you* believe it?"

"I don't know. If it's a game, it's a pretty pointless game. But if it's not, and somebody gets him because I wasn't there to stop it..."

"One more week, he said?"

"Yes."

"And that will be the end of it?"

"Like I said. One way or the other."

"Thank God."

I looked at her, just short of eyeballing. "I wish God *had* something to do with it, Laura. Until now, it's the Devil's own game we've been playing, and it seems there's no end to it."

"That leaves it up to you, then."

I took her hand and gently squeezed it. "I can always use a little help," I said. "From this side of Heaven."

I called Watusi the next morning and suggested that we meet for lunch at the Joe Louis Restaurant and Bar on 125th Street in Harlem. In earlier days, we'd have flipped a quarter to decide between Joe Louis' place and Jack Dempsey's, but now we just alternated between the two. I didn't give him a reason for the meeting, but I still had some lingering doubts about the fragile state of our friendship, and I was hoping for answers.

He was waiting for me in his favorite booth upstairs, by a big window overlooking 125th Street. He looked grim. And tired.

"What's the news?" I asked when I sat down.

"There seems to be none," he said.

"Same at my end, Tooss. How's Vip...How's Aabidullah holding up on his?"

"No complaints. Of course, he's beginning to feel the same sense of frustration that we are all experiencing. Have you a ready solution for that?"

"I might," I said.

"Have you considered the possibility that your Mr. Santini is quite insane?"

"That thought has occurred to me," I said. "Several times."

"Then why not call him on it?"

"I did. Just yesterday."

"I see."

I explained, he listened, and we ordered our lunch. Drinks arrived: a cold Schaefer for me, and an iced tea for him. For a long time, we didn't look at each other. He pretended to read the menu that he'd already ordered from, and I gazed blankly out at 125th Street.

"You didn't arrange this meeting just to talk about work, did you?" he said finally.

"No," I said. "I didn't."

"Is Aabidullah the subject?"

"No. You and me."

"You and *I*," he corrected, with a smile.

"You've gone off somewhere," I said. "Somewhere I can't go, and it bothers me some."

"Oh?"

"I feel like Santini. I know something is happening. I'm sure of it, but I don't know why."

"And what could happen?"

"We couldn't be friends anymore."

"And Aabidullah has something to do with it?"

"In a way. This Malcolm X he talks about, I read up about him in the newspaper the other day. There's no place in this world where he thinks colored people and white people can get along, or associate, or be friends."

"The term is 'black' now, not 'colored.' Remember?"

"Right. Sorry."

"Do you think *I* believe that, about blacks and whites? About us?"

"I'm the only white person you count as a friend, and you're the only black person who counts me as one."

"You're leaving out my white son-in-law, who I've come to appreciate over time. And you have my daughter on your side of the ledger, do you not?"

"You know what I mean, Tooss."

"Malcolm X does not hate white men who are fair and just. He hates whites who oppress black people, who want them to be their inferiors in all things. Who want them to be servile, if not slaves. He hates the people who hate, if you will. He hates them right back."

"Aabidullah. He hates me, and he's your friend. At some point, won't you have to choose between us?"

"Viper Robinson hates you for personal reasons, not reasons of race, Eddie. And Aabidullah is not the same person as Viper."

"But race was part of it."

"Jealousy was the larger part. You loved the woman he loved, and whom neither of you had the right to love, in that she was *my* woman. And when she died, Viper felt that both of us were responsible, because we weren't there to save her, and we could have been."

"But he doesn't hate you."

"It simmers some inside him, even toward me. You cannot be as angry a man as Viper was and still see with clear eyes."

"These last couple of months is when I've felt it the most," I said. "The distance between you and me."

He paused. The gleam in his eyes dimmed for a moment, then re-sparked. "Ah, that business," he said.

"Yes."

"That was internal business, Eddie. Personal business. You weren't supposed to notice -- or misinterpret -- it."

"I don't understand," I said.

"You aren't meant to. But if it means so much to you, I will do my best to smile at you more often. However, you will never get me to attend another of those infamous summer barbecues in lily-white Bensonhurst. Your three brothers-in-law are, quite frankly, intolerable."

"And that's got nothing to do with the fact that they're white?"

His smile widened. "You of all people, knowing them, must know that it has nothing to do with their color."

"That's an Amen," I said, just as our lunch arrived.

"And us?" I asked.

"Nothing has changed, otherwise."

"And what does that mean?"

"When the right time comes to answer that question, believe me, I will tell you," he said, and we finished our meal in silence.

Arnie and Liam were in the office when I returned from lunch, a minor mutiny that ended when I passed the word about my agreement with Santini. One more week, and that was it. We were done. Arnie was ready to quit at that very moment, despite his perpetual need for recreational money; but after some encouragement from Liam, he agreed to follow Maria Santini in her pink T-Bird for one more week. I spent the rest of the afternoon at home. After taking a well-deserved nap on the living room couch, I played with the girls and their dollhouses when Amanda came home from St. Margaret's and Mary awoke from her own nap. We read another chapter in *The Wind in the Willows* that night. Laura and I put the girls to bed at seven-thirty and had a late dinner together in front of the fireplace. Then I went back to work. I followed the Barracuda Brothers, and as usual, nothing extraordinary happened.

Until around midnight.

I'd followed them until then to their usual haunts, mostly bars and strip joints, and mostly in Uptown Manhattan and Brooklyn; but just before midnight they drove into Greenwich Village, stopping at 159 West 10th Street, where they parked and walked inside a bar called Julius'. Julius' was a well-known gathering place for homosexual men in the city. The Brothers would be as out of place there as Tibetan monks at a voodoo ceremony, so I wondered what their game was. I parked across the street and just watched for a while. A small but animated crowd was gathered around the entrance door, and in a few minutes the Brothers re-emerged, drinks in hand. After a few more minutes, they went back inside, lingering another half-hour. Then they came out again, spent another five absurd minutes on the sidewalk, and drove back to Santini's estate.

Laura was still awake when I got home. She asked me how the evening had gone.

I couldn't explain it to her.

11

The next morning, as always, Liam and Arnie were due to check in at the office before they followed their assigned suspects. We were all counting the days with eagerness now. But Arnie was late. So late, in fact, that I telephoned his apartment on Grand Concourse in the Bronx to see if he'd overslept. He didn't answer his phone, so Liam and I waited.

And waited.

He stormed in finally around nine-thirty, waving a copy of the *Daily News* in our astonished faces. "Have you seen this?" he asked excitedly. There was a young man standing behind him. "This here's my Marine buddy, Charlie," Arnie added hurriedly.

"Right," I said, frowning. "The one who's supposed to be watching the chauffeur while you're watching the daughter." I nodded in the man's direction. He could have been Arnie's brother except for his slighter build and the almost comic roundness of his face.

"Nice meeting you," said the man, but my full attention was still on Arnie.

"You gotta *look* at this, Eddie," he blurted again. "Page two."

"I do, do I? And where the hell have you been?"

"Read it, for Chrissake," said Arnie, thrusting the paper at me.

The headline read: SUSPICIOUS FATAL FIRE IN BROOKLYN. Rather than read further, I glared at him. "And?" I said.

"It's the chauffeur. That's his apartment that burned down. And they found a body inside."

"His?"

"Who else's? His was the only occupied apartment in the building."

I eyeballed Arnie's pal. "And?"

"I tailed him as usual all day yesterday," he explained. "Nothing special happened. Took the wife to the hairdresser and the bank. Took the limo to a car wash after he drove her home. He got back from Santini's around five-thirty, went up the stairs to his apartment, and he didn't come out again."

"Go on," I said.

"I stayed there another hour just to make sure he wasn't going anywhere after work, but it looked like he was in for the night, so I went home. I figured I'd wait until the next morning to follow him again. The fire started sometime after midnight, according to the newspaper, long after I was gone."

"Bad luck," I said.

"A hell of a lot more than bad luck, Eddie," said Arnie. Creating interruptions was one of Arnie's signature bad habits. "Well, *tell* him, Charlie. *Tell* the man."

"I showed up as usual around seven this morning. That's when he normally headed out for Santini's estate to start his workday. The hook-and-ladders were gone by then, but the arson squad was there in force. I didn't even have to ask. You could smell the gasoline in the air. The building was charred down to nothing. The fire got so hot that the top floor burned through and collapsed into the delicatessen underneath. They saved the buildings next to it, but just barely."

"Tell Eddie about the heat, Charlie," said Arnie, nudging him with a shoulder. "Go on. *Tell* him."

"Well, I talked to somebody from the arson squad. I guess he figured I was a reporter, although I didn't say I was. I asked him how hot the fire had been, and he said, 'Blue flame hot.' His exact words, honest to God. They found what was left of the guy in the rubble on the first floor. And they found two empty gasoline cans out back behind the building."

"So, the fire was deliberate."

"Damn straight. Somebody snuffed him," said Arnie.

"The chauffeur –- what was his name again?"

"Harry Appolino."

"And the address?"

"Right here in Bensonhurst. Bay Parkway. Only a couple of blocks from the Bath Avenue precinct station."

"That's Nick DeMassio's jurisdiction," I said, musing.

"Oh, shit." It was Arnie. A look of dismay was all over his face, and I knew why.

"And what's so bloody wrong with *him*?" asked Liam.

"I can't exactly go see Captain DeMassio at the moment," I said. "We're kind of not talking to each other."

"Understatement of the year," said Arnie, grinning as he lit a cigarette.

"That case last summer?" asked Liam.

"No, a different one. Back in February."

It was true enough. If I went anywhere near the Bath Avenue station house now, Captain Nicholas DeMassio would find a reason to put me in irons: spitting on the sidewalk, vagrancy, illegal parking, felony murder -- whatever charge he could pin on me. So, going to the police for anything now was out of the question.

"So, what's the plan, Eddie lad?" Liam asked.

"The morgue at Kings County Hospital," I said.

"Pickle?"

"He's the one."

Pickle, aka Paulie the Pickler, was a ghoulish, sallow-faced morgue attendant I had traded favors with over the years. He had no formal training in the mortuary arts, but he'd seen more than his share of dead bodies, and many of them not so pretty to look at. Normally, I would've had to get written permission from the Coroner's Office or the NYPD to access the details of any particular corpse's condition at the Kings County Morgue, but Nick DeMassio would make sure that didn't happen. Pickle could provide the end run I needed to get a closer look. It was all quite irregular, if not illegal, but Pickle and I had a nice arrangement going, and neither of us would to do anything to compromise it.

I drove straight to Kings County Hospital, sending Arnie and Liam back to their assignments and promising Arnie's Marine buddy that he'd be paid in full when the operation closed at the end of the week. I kind of envied him, with nobody to follow anymore. He could choose how to spend his time, which was a lot more than I could do. There was an NYPD black-and-white in the hospital parking lot, so I drove half a block further and left the Chrysler on Clarkson Avenue. Then I went looking for Paulie the Pickler in the morgue. He was standing outside the double doors that led to the cooler. Next to him were an assistant coroner, a pair of dark-suited detective lieutenants, and a uniformed officer. The cops were all Nick DeMassio's men, which meant that they were probably working on the arson fire on Bay Parkway. I waited at the end of the hall until their business was concluded, then waited a few moments more until the assistant coroner had gone back upstairs and Pickle was alone.

He had one of the drawers open when I walked into the cooler, leering intently at a refrigerated corpse. One of his hobbies. And if she were young and pretty, he might brush his hand softly across her cold face as he took in her nakedness.

"Hey, Eddie," he said, happening to look up. I was standing in the doorway.

"Morning, Pickle," I said.

"You wanna come look?" he asked, motioning with his free hand. "She's a real beauty. Sixteen years old. Except for those gashes on her wrists, she's perfect."

"No, thanks, Pickle," I said, frowning.

"Too bad," said Pickle, gently closing the drawer. "Anyways, I can always come back later. She just came in this morning. Her name's Jenny."

"Those cops who were just in here," I said, trying to deflect the conversation away from the cooler. "They're from Bath Avenue, aren't they?"

"Yup," said Pickle. "Arson fire in Bensonhurst."

"Did you happen to catch anything that was said?"

"Just an arson fire. Some guy burned up in it. Nothin' left of him except a lot o' scorched bones and a few scraps o' muscle tissue. One hell of a fire. Gasoline, they said."

"And the victim?"

"You really wanna see him? He's kinda hard to look at, even for me."

"In a minute, maybe," I said. "Anything on who he was?"

"The guy what lived there, I'm guessin'," said Pickle with a half-smile, as if a perfect idiot had asked the question.

"Is that who the cops think he is?"

"Not enough left of him to tell," said Pickle. "Swear to God. You still wanna look?"

"In a minute. So, what *did* the cops think? What did the assistant coroner think?"

He paused to consider an unwelcome thought. "Well, maybe you *should* look, then."

He moved down the line of drawers, pulled one open, drew the sheet from the body, and stepped back.

I stepped forward. I looked into the drawer. And I reeled back from it.

"Jesus!" I said. "What the hell happened to his skull?"

"There ain't one," said Pickle. "Not really, anyway. Nothin' much left. Just a bunch of little pieces that *used* to be a skull. What was left of him ended up on the floor of the deli downstairs. Burned to a crisp. You can still make out the shape of the body, sort of, but the cops didn't find much of a skull. Cops figure somebody bashed his head in first, and then set the place on fire. Cops found an ax head not far away from the body. They figure somebody bashed his skull into little tiny pieces with an ax, and then the wood handle burned up in the fire. Cops said the ax head was still white-hot when they found it. They found little pieces of skull, parts of eye sockets, parts of a jaw, and teeth, scattered around the body. So, like I said, somebody did a number on him upstairs, set the fire, the floor caved in, and his body ended up on the first floor, in the deli."

"And they don't know who he is?"

"They *gotta* know. Who else would it be? The guy what lived there. You know the guy?"

"No."

"I'll tell you one thing. If it ain't a homicide, then I never seen one," said Pickle. "Somebody had a real hard-on for this guy."

"Looks that way."

"Anything else I can do for ya, Eddie?"

"Don't tell the police I was here. Especially not the Bath Avenue cops." I slipped him a fiver.

"My lips, they're sealed tight, Eddie."

"That's good, Pickle."

"Oh, yeah, and there's one more thing. I kind of overheard the cops talkin' to each other out in the hall when they didn't know I was listenin'. Somethin' about lookin' for a guy who came out from behind some buildin' after a fire."

"They say who?"

"Nope. Just some guy."

"And they were talking about *this* case? About the arson fire?"

"Only big fire I heard of lately, but I don't know. Like I said, they was just talkin' shop. Might have been somethin' happened years and years ago. Maybe they was just reminiscin'."

I turned to leave.

"See you later, Pickle. Give me a call if you hear anything more. There's another fiver for you if you do."

"Sure, Eddie, sure. Hey, you sure you don't wanna look at this other one? She's a real beauty."

"No, thanks. You can look for me."

"I hope they don't send her off to a funeral home too quick. That'd be a real shame."

He looked like he was ready to say something else, but I'd already closed the double doors protectively behind me.

12

I drove to Santini's estate, hoping to find Liam's car at the curb outside. He was halfway up the block, parked under a large, leafy elm tree; but he was still close enough to see who drove past those big cast-iron gates. I couldn't see Arnie's car. Maybe that meant that Maria and the pink T-Bird were loose in the city. It almost didn't matter at this stage. Because the rules of engagement had changed. Quite literally overnight. One of the people Jimmy Santini thought wanted to kill him was now dead. One of our seven suspects was now a murder victim. It was like one of the Borgias trying to poison somebody and then getting a fatal dose himself. It was like Julius Caesar stabbing Brutus.

I parked about five spaces behind Liam and took a moment to admire Santini's little fiefdom. What palace intrigues were afoot inside? What new conspiracies were hatching? And what was Santini's role in all this? Was the fox now chasing the hounds? Were my operatives and I all pawns in a lethal game of Santini's design? I'd thought until now that Santini was at the very least paranoid and possibly on the edge of early senility, but those thoughts were giving way quickly to new and more frightening ones. I began to worry about Laura and my two little girls. Perhaps it was time for them to visit their Uncle Johnny Temafonte in Detroit again. Perhaps I should keep my .38 closer at hand. Under the pillow, even. I was going down Alice's rabbit hole again, and the thought struck me that, once inside, I might not find my way out this time.

Liam saw me approaching in the rear view mirror. He didn't speak when I opened the passenger side door and sat down. He turned his good ear in my direction.

"Anything doing?" I asked.

"Nope. Come to keep me company, then?"

"Change of plans. I want you to skip the surveillance for today and find out whatever you can on Harry Appolino."

"Santini's dead chauffeur?"

"Yes. Can you handle it?"

"Sure enough, lad."

"Good. Find out what you can about him."

"Didn't your spic snitch already cover that subject?"

"He did."

"And he didn't find a bleedin' thing about the bloke, if I remember right."

"That's why I need you to look. I want you to find out everything and anything on this guy. Start with the city and telephone directories at the main library, then go over to Motor Vehicles, Borough Hall, wherever. Look up every damn Appolino in the city. All five boroughs. Maybe we'll find something. Maybe not."

"And maybe I'll just go back to bleedin' Dublin for a visit. After I get my pay, don't you know? I'm overdue for a bleedin' vacation."

"You'll get it," I said.

I went home for a quick lunch with Laura and Mary. I said nothing about the new concerns, but Laura could see that something wasn't right with me.

"Want to tell me what's on your mind?" she asked after she'd tucked Mary in for her afternoon nap.

"Nothing's wrong. Actually, I'm kind of relieved. I mean, now that this Santini business is almost over."

"Less than a week to go, right?"

"Five more days, yes."

"Well, it must be something else, then, mustn't it?"

"Something *else*?"

The look she gave me was more piercing than petulant. And she followed that with the smile she always offered whenever she had the advantage of me. "If it isn't something else, then why did Captain DeMassio just call?"

"Nick DeMassio?"

"The same. From the Bath Avenue precinct station. He expects you to be there shortly, by the way."

"Not a social call, then?"

"Hardly. And, if you take too much time getting over there, he'll send a pair of uniformed officers in a black-and-white, 'lights a-flashing,' as he put it, to fetch you."

"Oh," I said.

"You can tell me about it when you get home," she said with a fixed grin. "*If* you get home. At the very least, if they decide to keep you, I can probably post your bail."

I announced myself to the desk sergeant on the first floor and went up the stairs to DeMassio's office on the second. Having no windows, it looked and felt like a cell. DeMassio had always looked trapped in it, caged. Never the carefree type, he'd been happier by far as a detective-lieutenant and, before that, as a uniformed cop in my neighborhood. He seemed to have only one fixed expression of late: suppressed anger.

"Afternoon, Nick," I said as pleasantly as possible. "You wanted to see me?"

"You were at the city morgue this mornin'," he growled. "I wanna know why." There was a wooden chair next to his gunmetal desk, but he waved me away when I tried to sit in it. "And you'll tell me standin' up," he said.

"Who said I was there?" I said.

"You were already skatin' on thin ice when you walked in here, Eddie. Don't push your luck."

"You called *me*, Nick."

"And it's '*Captain* DeMassio,' as far as you're concerned. Don't you forget it."

"Listen, Nick -- *Captain* -- about that misunderstanding back in February, it wasn't my fault. I…"

"Why were you at the morgue? Why were you talkin' with Paulie the Pickler? I want straight answers."

"A case I'm working on," I said.

"Is that a fact? And what case is that?"

"Sorry, Nick. That's privileged information."

"Oh, is it? Listen up, Eddie. You are one perpetual pain in the ass who might soon be losin' his shamus license, but you're not fuckin' Perry Mason. Between you and the NYPD, nothin's privileged."

"I already lost my license once. Remember?"

"And you're workin' on an encore. Am I clear?"

"Clear enough," I said. "And so?"

"There's only one stiff that might interest you at the morgue right now. Only one. Process of elimination. It's the arson victim, right? So, what's your interest?"

"Privileged information, Nick."

"Who hired you?"

"Privileged information."

DeMassio strolled to the windowless back wall and the water cooler. When he came back, the paper cup held tightly in his hand, he sat down again.

"Heard a rumor you're maybe workin' for Jimmy Santini. Hired a whole bunch of extra guys to keep tabs on his family. Am I right?"

"No comment, Nick."

"The reason I'm askin' is: that arson fire over on Bay Parkway. The victim, he was Santini's chauffeur. He's the stiff you went to ask about in the morgue. And if you *are* workin' for his boss, if you *are* workin' for one of the biggest murderin' hoods in Brooklyn, I wanna know why. Holdin' back information on a capital murder case can get you some jail time. And a suspension of your shamus license. You better come clean this time, Eddie."

I took the wooden chair without asking and sat in it. "All right," I said. "But what I say doesn't leave this office, or maybe I'm a dead man."

DeMassio winced. "Son of a bitch. So he *did* hire you."

"I'll tell you the details on one condition."

"And that is?"

"A trade of information. I tell you something, you tell me something. Something I won't read about in the *Daily News* tomorrow."

"Like what?"

"The guy at the fire. Outside, in the alley. Who is he?"

"You know about him?"

"Not enough to be useful."

"And if I tell you..."

"Then I'll tell you about me and Santini. If there's anything to tell."

DeMassio took a second trip to the cooler, but he didn't have a paper cup with him on his return trip. He sat down. He leaned forward. "If I hear this on the street, Eddie...if I hear this even outside this room, you're gonna do some time for havin' loose lips. Hard time. Am I makin' myself clear?"

"Clear enough."

"Okay, then. The fire started around midnight. Naturally, the whole neighborhood came out to watch. Nobody saw anybody or anything out o' the ordinary when the fire started, and by two in the mornin', most of the gawkers had gone back to bed. But two guys were still out there. They saw somebody come from the back of the building about that time. Not a good enough look for a detailed description, but they saw him. There's no access behind the building to the next street over, so there's only one way that somebody could get to the front o' that building from out back where the gasoline cans were found, and that was down the alley. Like I said, all this happens a couple of hours after the fire was first reported. Who woulda been behind the building all that time if not the guy who set the fire? And why did he wait so long to make his getaway?"

"Maybe he's a pyro," I said. "Those guys like to watch whatever they set on fire. That's how they get their kicks."

"Sure, but they do it from a safe place. The area outside the building was still hot halfway across the street, with burnin' debris all over the place. Even the firemen couldn't get too close. Then, two hours later, like I said, this guy runs down the alley from behind the building and disappears."

"Did any of the firemen see him?"

"Nope. Just those two guys. Anyway, he's the one we're lookin' for. I'm thinkin' maybe he waited too long after he started the fire, and then he couldn't get to the alley and make his escape until the fire cooled down. That, or he was afraid people on the street would see him if he tried it any sooner. He must've hid out someplace behind the building where the heat and smoke from the fire couldn't get at him. The two witnesses who saw him come out, they've agreed not to talk about the guy to the newspapers or anybody else. That's our ace in the hole findin' him if he doesn't know that we're lookin'. Okay? That's my part of the bargain. Now it's your turn."

When I was through explaining, he grinned. It was the most almost-friendly look he'd given me in two months, but I knew it didn't change anything.

"So, you think Santini's tryin' to knock off all his suspects before they knock him off?"

"I don't know, Nick."

"From what I know of him, it's a possibility."

"I know him, too," I said.

"And why would he want to knock off his chauffeur? If he didn't like the guy, or if he thought he couldn't trust him, he coulda just fired him. Why kill him? Why burn him up?"

"And why crush his skull in the process?"

"That, too."

"So, you see my problem," I said.

"Times seven."

"Six, now. Any ideas?"

"Maybe. We could try leaning on some of Santini's soldiers, bring 'em in one at a time, see who maybe had a hard-on for the chauffeur. Or see if one of them knows somethin'."

"Even if they know something, they're not about to tell us."

"Okay. Not a good idea. And you're givin' it one more week?"

"Five days. That's what Santini agreed to. Then it's done, one way or the other."

"Santini's word isn't worth a damn. You oughta know that, Eddie. I can put a protective tail on you if you like."

"I know how to watch my own back, Nick."

For a moment, he seemed to relax into his chair, his big frame losing some of its practiced stiffness. "Okay," he said. "Do it your own way."

"I plan to," I said.

"Maybe the situations are related, and maybe they're not. You keep mum about the guy in the alley, and I won't make it known that you're workin' with me. Hell, Santini probably knows it anyway."

"That's what I'm afraid of," I said.

"Well, keep in touch."

"Sure. Friends again?" I asked.

His big frame stiffened. "We'll see," he said. "If you're still alive when this is all over."

13

Rather than go home and absorb more sarcasm from Laura, I went to the main branch of the Brooklyn Public Library on Grand Army Plaza. Liam, as ordered, was already looking through the city directories and the telephone books, but he didn't look happy in his work. I thought he might cut into me with a sardonic limerick or two when he saw me, but he just glowered.

"Any luck?" I said.

"Too fookin' much, Eddie lad. These Appolinos, they must breed like rabbits. Must be twenty in Brooklyn alone."

"That's not so bad," I said. "Twenty people."

"That's twenty fookin' *households*, Eddie."

"Okay. So...."

"And what are you doin' here, anyways? I thought this dee-lightful assignment was mine alone."

"Just killing time. I'll pick up the Barracuda Brothers again tonight."

"Anything there?"

I laughed, and somebody at the next table shushed me. "You won't believe it," I said, "but they went to Julius' last night."

"The fag bar?"

"The very same place."

"Gettin' open-minded, are they?"

"I doubt it. More likely, they'd go in just to bust heads. Anyway, I'll find out tonight what they're up to. Maybe."

"And does your dear wife know how you're spendin' your nights lately?"

"I hope the hell not."

"She open-minded, then?"

I didn't answer.

I parked outside the Santini estate just after dark and waited for the Barracuda Brothers to begin their evening's adventures. For a while I had the radio turned on, hoping to hear some Sinatra or Tony Bennett. Instead I got a steady diet of Brenda Lee, Del Shannon, and Elvis Presley. I couldn't be bothered to change the channel, so I turned off the radio. It was just another part of the pattern of dissatisfaction that seemed to be the norm lately. I hadn't had the time to check with my operatives on the activities of our other prime suspects, but I wasn't expecting much. As for the Barracuda Brothers, I still couldn't believe that they would turn so violently against the man they called Pop. It was the name I'd used to address my own father, and I was just short of certain that they felt about their Pop the same way I'd felt about mine. Still, Santini had put them on his suspect list, and he was paying me to keep close tabs on them.

Until the end of the week.

A light rain started falling around seven. A genuine spring rain, not a deluge, and not an ice storm. I'd already had a day full of unpleasant surprises, so I was giving the Brothers only until nine to show themselves. After that, I was going home to bed and not getting up until I felt like it. Another five days more and I could say the hell with the whole thing, including Nick DeMassio's part in it. He was at least speaking to me again, and if I didn't find any new ways to piss him off, we might actually be semi-friends at some point. Time would tell.

It was just eight when the Brothers finally drove through the opened gates of Santini's estate in the same black Pontiac that had taken me that first time out to Wantaugh and the Jones Beach Hotel. They surprised me by going directly to Julius' and quickly disappearing inside. I had a good view of the entrance where I was parked, and so I watched the colorful tableaux of characters that had assembled on the sidewalk just outside. I didn't care if they preferred boys to girls. I considered myself open-minded, even though I wasn't. Like Watusi and Viper when it came to white guys, and Gino when it came to beatniks, I felt somehow both apart from the clientele at Julius' and superior to them. I was about to place my hat on the seat next to me when Rico, approaching from behind, poked a .38 at me through the driver's side window and said, "Evenin', Lombardi. Wanna go for a ride?"

"I'm waiting for my date," I said, grinning. "He's a big tall one with ringlets and dressed like Shirley Temple."

"We'd rather have ya take a ride with us for a while," said Rico. "Is this here .38 enough persuasion for ya?"

"It'll have to do," I said, and got out of the car. Carmine was only a few steps behind me. He nudged me roughly into the passenger seat of the Pontiac and took the seat in back. Rico took the driver's seat, and we pulled away from the curb.

"Back entrance?" I asked.

"Surprised ya, huh? Don't you ever read the Fire Code, Lombardi? Every place o' business has to have one."

"So that two straight Eye-talian guys like you, pretending to be with the queer crowd, can get away without being spotted? That's assuming, of course that you aren't already part of that crowd."

Carmine scowled, but Rico smiled at me from behind the wheel. "That's funny, Lombardi," said Rico. "Hey, Carmine, don't you think that's funny?"

"Yeah. Funny," said Carmine, and we drove.

At first, I thought we might be going to Wantaugh again. Maybe Santini -- Pop -- wanted another of those pleasant chats we'd been having. Maybe he'd decided for some reason to take the Brothers off his list. But when they chose the off-road that would take us to the swamps and marshes around Floyd Bennett Field, I thought differently. I didn't bother to ask where we were going now. I knew. And I knew it wasn't just going to be a warning. It was *that* kind of ride. I found myself falling silent, any wisecrack I might have tried out on them drying up in my throat. It was Carmine, in the back seat, who broke the silence.

"You remember the business with that motherfucker Scarpetti back in '49, Lombardi?" Carmine said. "You remember that?"

"Sure he does," chimed in Rico. "We saved his fuckin' ass. On the Brooklyn Bridge. You remember that, Lombardi? You was hangin' off the Brooklyn Bridge."

"And we saved your fuckin' ass," said Carmine. "From that crazy broad with the .45. You remember that?"

"How could he not remember that?" said Rico.

"Absolutely. You was usin' up your last few minutes on this earth, and we saved your fuckin' ass, Lombardi."

"Saved your fuckin' ass," echoed Rico.

"Yes," I said. "I remember."

"I mean, Jesus, Carmine! We save this guy's fuckin' ass, and now he's followin' us around. Like we's criminals or somethin'."

"Yeah. Followin' us around. Like we was criminals, for Chrissake. Can you believe it?"

"And maybe thinkin' we're also a coupla fags. Two All-American boys like us, and Lombardi thinks we dress up like ballerinas or somethin' when Pop's not lookin'. And after we saved his fuckin' ass and all. Jesus!"

"He's gonna wanna tell us somethin' different now," said Rico. "Any minute now. I just know he is."

"Any minute."

"But we know he's gonna be a fuckin' liar. Ain't that right?"

"Right as rain," said Carmine. "A fuckin' liar who wants to save his worthless ass."

"Absolutely."

"So, maybe it's better if he don't say nothin'. Might even live a coupla minutes longer if he don't say nothin'."

"Nothin' at all."

"Yup, better off keepin' his lyin' mouth shut now."

"One hundred percent," said Rico.

Those were my cues, and I took them.

Dirt roads of varying widths crisscrossed the bogs and marshes that bordered Floyd Bennett Field. A dozen or more access points to places untraveled by and unknown to any but the very few who knew how to navigate them in the dark, with the headlights turned off. Out here, in the Mob's vast, hidden cemetery, a car was always lighter on the way out than on the way in. It was nearly soundless in the dark wilderness that surrounded us -- there were no commercial flights out of Floyd Bennett anymore -- but there was a steady drone of air traffic from Idlewild just to the northeast across Jamaica Bay. This was where they buried the bodies, all right, but who'd given the order to dispatch me? Santini? Or had the Barracuda Brothers their own reason for taking me on this last ride? Had I been so wrong about them? Had my instincts been so mistaken that I hadn't seen this coming? I tried to think of a strategy that would work against sheer dim-wittedness, but none came to me. Carmine had the gun muzzle of his .38 hard against the nape of my neck.

Rico stopped the car. The dirt road was so narrow that the low-hanging branches of small trees and shrubs brushed against it. It was utterly black all around us, but the Brothers knew where we were. They knew this place, all right, almost as if they had its coordinates on a map. It was Carmine who spoke first, breaking the long silence, repeating himself from earlier.

"We saved your fuckin' ass, Lombardi, back there on the Brooklyn Bridge. Back in '49. Saved you from that fuckin' vixen with the .45. And then we find out about *this*. This thing you've been doin'. We're fuckin' insulted. You know what I mean?"

"Fuckin' insulted," echoed Rico.

"What exactly is *this*?" I asked finally. "What the hell did I do that you boys want to kill me for it?"

"He's gonna lie to us again," said Rico. "I just know it."

"Won't do him any good," said Carmine.

"Well, Lombardi? What's it gonna be?"

I fooled the both of them by opening the door quickly and stepping out into the darkness.

"If you're going to kill me, stop whining and do it," I said, standing my ground and glaring at them. The sound of my voice told them where I was, but I didn't care.

They followed, slowly. Two .38s were probably on me now. Two disembodied voices spoke to each other in the void.

"Well, Carmine, whatta ya think?"

"Well, if he wants it that bad..."

"We could certainly grant his wish," said Carmine.

"Where *should* we shoot him?" asked Rico. "In the head's good. It's quick, anyway. A little messy, but...the heart, maybe?"

"The balls," said Carmine. "Let's shoot him in the balls. No, better yet, *between* the balls."

"Shoot him in his *dick*? Is that manly? Hell, I can barely see his fuckin' head and he's right in front o' me. Light a match, will ya? Or get the flashlight from the trunk."

"Oh, yeah," said Carmine. "Almost forgot."

"You wanna tell us now, Lombardi?" said Rico when Carmine went to open the trunk. "We know already, so you might as well just say it. Tell the truth. Die with a clear conscience."

"He's right, Lombardi. Confession's good for the soul. That's what the priest says."

"Hey, where's the fuckin' flashlight?" Carmine howled out of the dark.

"Under the shovel."

"Okay, I got it," said Carmine. I heard him shuffling toward me in the near pitch dark. He shined the strong light in my face.

"Last chance, Lombardi," said Rico.

"He's not answerin'," said Carmine, and pointed the light at just below my belt.

"Okay, then. Here goes!" shouted Rico, and fired the gun. When the echo faded, I was still alive, and they were still standing in front of me.

Grinning like Alice's cat.

"See? I *told* ya!" shouted Rico. "He *flinched*! That's ten bucks you owe me."

"He didn't flinch."

"He damn well did!"

"Didn't!"

"Did! I saw him."

"Well, *I* didn't see him flinch," said Carmine. "And if I didn't see him, it didn't happen."

"That's 'cause you didn't look. I *looked*."

"The hell you did!"

"You owe me ten bucks."

"Why don't we ask Lombardi?"

"Hey, Lombardi, ya flinched, didn't ya? I know ya did."

"Lombardi?"

"Jesus, say somethin', will ya?"

"Jesus. You don't really think we was gonna kill ya, do ya?" said Carmine with a smile.

"I think he does," said Rico. "Look at the way he's lookin' at ya. He really, honest-to-God thinks so."

"Nah, we wasn't gonna kill ya, Lombardi. We was just fuckin' with ya. On account o' you and Pop."

"But ya *did* flinch, didn't ya? Come on, Lombardi. Come clean. It's worth a sawbuck to me."

Carmine was closest, so I hit him first.

14

"Jesus!" whined Carmine, looking up at me in astonishment from the dirt road. "You don't have to go and get sore about it. We was only fuckin' with ya." Rico was half-upright against the side of the Pontiac, nursing his bruised chin.

"Just fuckin' with ya, that's all."

"On account o' you and Pop."

I glared at them.

"Okay, so maybe ya *don't* know why we was fuckin' with ya," said Rico. "But Pop, he thinks we wanna kill him, and we don't, so... You really oughta know about that, Lombardi. 'Cause *we* do."

"We *know*, Lombardi."

"Know *what*?" I asked.

"You meetin' with Pop, and him thinkin' that we was gonna kill him."

"It ain't so," said Carmine. "We love Pop, kind of."

"Who told you this?" I asked finally.

"Nobody. We told *ourselves*. We found out."

"You and Pop. At the Jones Beach Hotel."

"That isn't possible," I said.

"Yeah, well it is. Tell the man, Carmine."

"Let's tell him on the way back," said Carmine. "This place gives me the creeps."

"He's right, ya know," said Rico. "You move five feet in any direction, and you're steppin' on somebody."

We were halfway to Flatlands before Carmine began his narration. "Pop's been cheatin' on our stepmother. Out at the Jones Beach Hotel. We know because we followed him out there a coupla times. We called him on it, which didn't make him too happy, and things got kinda hot and heavy there for a while. Maybe he thinks that's why we wanna kill him. But we *don't*. Not that much, anyway. But it was a lousy thing t' do, what he was doin', and we was gonna make him stop it, okay? We hired this guy, see. Electronics guy. He lives in Wantaugh. We rented the room next to where Pop does his fuckin', and this electronics guy set up a tape recorder in there. Right next to the vent. One o' those VMs, ya know. Voice o' Music. Real nice machine. Any time we thought Pop was goin' out to that hotel to get laid, or for any other reason -- he usually takes one o' the other cars, and he usually goes alone -- we called this guy up, had him drive over there ahead of Pop, and had him record the whole thing."

"How'd your man get past the desk clerk without notice? My understanding was that your father figured to be the only tenant when he was there."

"Actually, there's three of 'em."

"And?"

"We told 'em we'd blow their fuckin' heads off if Pop ever found out."

"All right," I said. "Go on."

"We figured Pop'd quit it if we threatened to play the tapes for our stepmom, but he didn't even care. He said she already knew. Anyway, one o' the times we had this guy recordin' what was goin' on in that hotel room, he recorded you and Pop."

"Just the once?" I asked.

Carmine grinned. "No. You was there another time, when you chased the bimbo out. We heard that little talk, too. You're lucky you walked out alive from that one. Never heard nobody talk to Pop like that before. Even we wouldn't do it. Anyway, we figured we had a right t' fuck with ya, on account o' you thinkin' we'd do anything to hurt Pop. And we can tell ya right now: if Pop thinks somebody's out t' ice him, then somebody's out t' ice him."

"His wife, maybe? Your stepmother?"

"Lots o' folks got reasons. Pop, he ain't no saint."

"But family? Inner circle?"

"What's *that* mean, inner circle?"

"People close to him," I said.

"Don't know nothin' about that," said Carmine, "but if somebody tries to get at Pop, it's not gonna be us."

"All right," I said. "Maybe I'll buy what you're saying. But I still have a question. Were you two -- as you say -- just fucking with me when you let me follow you to Julius'?"

"Oh, that," said Rico. "Pop's lawyer, Fanucci, he's queer. Pop knows it. Makes fun of him in public any chance he gets."

"And the lawyer's a suspect."

"Yeah. So while you was busy trackin' *us*, we was trackin' the fag lawyer. Once in a while, anyway, when we wasn't doin' other stuff. If that Fanucci guy tries anything against Pop, we'll be on him like glue. So how come *you* don't know 'bout him? Don't you got somebody on *his* ass, too?"

"Yes, and no," I said. The lawyer was Aabidullah's assignment, but only during daylight hours, as per my own orders. Aurelio Rodriguez should have known, should have told me that afternoon at Nero's, but he'd missed it. I figured I was due a partial refund on my hundred dollars, not that he would ever willingly give it up.

"You oughta see him in there, the little bald-headed fag," said Carmine. "Dresses up like Bo Peek sometimes."

"That's Bo *Peep*," I said.

"Actually, we never really seen him 'cept in a cheap lookin' suit."

Before I knew it, we were back in front of Julius'. Rico pulled to the curb, but he left the motor running.

"Does he know you're there watching him?" I said.

"Sure. He don't care. He's got a swell job with Pop. We could laugh in his face, call him a fag, and he'd laugh right back -- and keep rakin' in the dough."

"You wanna check him out inside?" asked Rico "The lawyer, I mean."

"Another time, maybe."

"If you come dressed as a sheep, and he's in there, you'd better watch your ass," said Carmine, and they laughed.

"Get it?" said Rico. "Watch your *ass*?"

"I got it," I said. I stepped out of the Pontiac. The same colorful crowd was outside Julius'. "Thanks for the ride," I said.

"Let's do it again sometime," said Rico, grinning.

"Just remember, Lombardi. We're on Pop's side, just like you," said Carmine.

"Just like you," said Rico.

"We ain't kiddin'."

"I'll try to remember that," I said. I took another step back. The Pontiac looked less like a hearse now, but I wanted to be away from it. Far away.

I wasn't ready to go home. It's not every day you nearly get yourself planted in the marshes of Floyd Bennett Field, so I opted for a cold Schaefer at the Tip Top Tavern. I didn't recognize the bartender, but then I wasn't used to coming here at midnight. In my younger days, my bachelor days, this would have been my place of refuge in times of crisis, professionally or otherwise. Times when the blues seemed to stay with you twenty-four hours a day, seven days a week. Times when a stiff drink or two or three seemed like the right answer to whatever was going wrong.

I almost didn't see him at first, sitting in that dark corner of the bar. His head was on the table, and there were two empty bottles of J.T.S. Brown and a half-filled glass next to him. I cast a fierce glance at the bartender, and then I ran straight to Aurelio. I felt his pulse first. It was an odd thing to do, but somehow I knew he wasn't just drunk. The doctors at the charity hospital had told him that alcohol was the same as poison now. I'd been so sure he'd stay on the wagon, so sure that 7-Up had replaced J.T.S. Brown as his beverage of choice, but I'd been wrong.

"Aurelio," I said, shaking him, looking close at his rheumy eyes. "You okay? You okay, *amigo*?"

He didn't answer. And he didn't move.

The bartender was looking over with detached amusement. *"Call an ambulance!"* I shouted. He looked at me as if he hadn't heard a word, and he walked casually to the middle of the bar. The phone was at the far end.

"Call a goddamn ambulance!" I shouted again, and this time he moved back to the end of the bar where the phone was. I took a

quick look at Aurelio, at the two empty liquor bottles, and my insides churned. He had a pulse, but not much of one, and his breathing was labored.

"Come on, *amigo*," I said, shaking him again. "Look at me."

"You want me to make him some coffee?" asked the bartender.

"He's way past coffee, pal," I said, pushing against my anger. "How long's he been in here?"

"Couple of hours."

"And he bought both bottles here?"

"Brought one in with him, half empty. I sold him the other one. He's been in here before. Used to drink 7-Up all the time. I told him I can't make no money sellin' him 7-Ups. Said he oughta be drinkin' a man's drink."

"So, you know him."

"Sure," he said, and smiled.

"You sold him *poison*, you sonofabitch. You know that?"

"That's good stuff," he said, stiffening. "That's J.T.S. Brown."

"Well, it's fucking poison to an alcoholic. Did he look like he could handle it?"

"I just sell the stuff, mister," he said. "I ain't nobody's big brother." He started wiping down the bar, which was his own little way of saying, "Fuck you."

"Well, I hope you're here tomorrow, pal," I said. "Because I'm coming back to kick your worthless ass."

"Yeah, yeah," he said.

Aurelio stirred slightly, groaning.

"You okay, *amigo*? It's me. Eddie."

"*Buenos noches*," he said, and spit up. I stuck my finger down his throat and kept it there until he threw up on the table. Then I did it again. And once more after that. There was no color to his face. I turned back to the bartender. "You *gonna call or not?*"

"Sure, sure," he said. "I'll *call* already."

I turned back to Aurelio. "What the hell happened, *amigo*? Why'd you fall off the wagon?"

"Just a little relapse. *Un poco.*"

"I'm closin' soon," the bartender announced. "And you'd better clean up that mess before I do."

My fists were still balled tight when the ambulance arrived. They took Aurelio to Lower Manhattan Hospital on Stuyvesant Square and put him in a bed in the charity ward. He'd been there before, almost died there before, but it looked like this time might really be his last. I waited for a while outside the ward. There was a public telephone there, and so I called Laura. She wouldn't be happy knowing I'd been at a bar at midnight instead of in bed next to her, but I'd given up lying to her a long time ago. I told her it would be a while, until I thought Aurelio was out of danger, before I came home. That was three in the morning, just before he'd slipped into a coma. I left an hour later, when there was still no change.

I got up late the next morning, but there was still time to check on Aurelio at Lower Manhattan Hospital before heading to the office and going through the final motions of the surveillance operation.

"Just four more days before it's all over," I said to Laura, bleary-eyed. She was pouring coffee. My two eggs, over easy, were looking up at me from the kitchen table. Looking with purpose.

"It's four too many," she said.

"I had to stay with Aurelio," I said. "I know it's late in the game, but I'm just now figuring out how much I owe him."

She smiled. "In back wages?"

"In how many times his information made my job a little easier, or maybe saved my life."

"Then that's where you belonged last night," she said, "and that's where you should be now."

It was a clear morning. Spring was fully upon the Borough. A warm breeze was blowing off the ocean. I got to the hospital before visiting hours, but when a nurse tried to dissuade me, I stormed past her into the charity ward. Aurelio's bed had been made. He wasn't in it.

I knew what that meant.

15

My first instinct was to return to the Tip Top Tavern and beat the bartender to a pulp, but he would be off-duty now, so I slunk into the office and checked with my answering service. Between yesterday morning and this one, I'd had only two calls, one from an office supply company, and the other from Watusi. I called his number, but he didn't answer, so I went down to the Bella Italia Luncheonette, grabbed a Coke and a newspaper, climbed the stairs, and waited.

Arnie wandered in well past lunchtime, carrying a delicatessen bag.

"What are you doing here?" I asked with some annoyance. "You're supposed to be eating your lunch in your car and keeping track of Santini's daughter."

"Not a problem," said Arnie. "The princess, she's done all the stuff she's gonna do today. It's her pattern. That's what you want me to do, isn't it? Get familiar with her pattern?"

"Daytime patterns don't tell us anything about what she does at night," I said, and explained about the lawyer and Julius'.

"No shit?" said Arnie. "*That* place?"

"That place, partner."

"I'll be damned."

"So, follow her at least a couple of evenings for a while."

"Like tonight?" he asked, frowning.

"No time like the present."

"Okay," he said, pouring himself a cup of coffee. "Suits me. Anyway, end of the week and we're done, right?"

"You got it right," I said. "And how's your Marine buddy?"

"Antsy for his pay."

"So are we all," I said. "He'll get paid when we all do."

"And the dead chauffeur?"

"I've got Liam checking on him. So far, nothing. But Captain DeMassio knows what we're up to. That means we have to play everything close to the vest from now on. I don't know if he's got a bunch of plainclothes cops keeping tabs on us, but we aren't in a position to hold anything back from him. If he asks, officially or otherwise, we tell him."

"And the wife? The one Liam was watchin'?"

"Nothing out of the ordinary yet. Go home, eat your lunch, and then follow the white-gloved young lady in the T-Bird from around five to after midnight. Let's see what she does, if anything."

"Mind if I finish my coffee first?" he said.

"You mean *my* coffee? Hit the road, Arnie."

The phone rang as Arnie was walking out. He stopped as if to linger and listen in, but I waved him out the door. Watusi was on the line.

"What's up, Tooss?" I said.

"I have news from Aabidullah," he said.

"Can't we just call him Viper, out of earshot?"

"You sound testy."

"I *am* testy."

"Santini's lawyer, Fanucci. A woman visited him yesterday afternoon at his office near Borough Hall. Aabidullah thinks the woman was Santini's wife, based on her description. The 'middle-aged white bitch,' as he calls her. If it *was* Santini's wife, Aabidullah wants to know why your Mr. O'Rourke failed to follow her there."

"I took Liam off her that morning. Sorry. Bad timing."

"Aabidullah then took it upon himself to find out a bit more about the man. Did you know what his expertise was before he came to be Santini's -- what is the term -- mouthpiece?"

"No idea," I said.

"Divorce law. Mr. Fanucci specialized in keeping potentially high-profile divorce proceedings out of the headlines. Aabidullah found the information in one of those legal directories at the public library."

"And?"

"Aabidullah did a bit more snooping. A look at the court calendar. It seems that the divorce process has been progressing for some time. Santini and his wife are in final negotiations for a settlement."

"And?"

"Aabidullah believes, and I concur, that it would be foolish in the extreme for Mrs. Santini to think of murdering her husband now. His murder would tie the settlement process in legal knots for an indeterminate time, basically until the District Attorney could decide with some certainty that Santini's wife had *not* been involved in the death of her husband. Convicted murderers cannot inherit from their victims."

"So?"

"So, Aabidullah and I agree that spending any more time on Mrs. Santini would be a waste of both time and energy."

"That's not his territory, and it's not his call," I said with some heat. "The *lawyer* is his territory. So, tell him to keep at it."

"And my charge? The psychiatrist. Does it continue?"

"Anything new with him?"

"His professional life has been quite busy of late. A steady stream of clients, all driving very nice cars. Other than that and two-hour lunches at some of the better restaurants near his home and office and his trips to the gym, there is very little to report. It would seem that we are running out of suspects, or that they are all the *wrong* suspects. Would you agree?"

"Something could still happen."

"You're becoming an optimist, then?"

"Four days and we're done," I said.

"A minor eternity, is it not?" he said, and hung up on me.

The last four days passed quietly. Like a fading echo. Like a bad dream finally going away. I paid for Aurelio's funeral expenses and bought him a plot in St. John Cemetery in Queens. The hired gravedigger and I were the only ones at graveside. Alcoholics Anonymous was supposed to send somebody out, but nobody showed. The monument company I used said it would be a month before his permanent marker would be in place. There was no date of birth on the temporary marker. Nobody in any of the public offices of the Five Boroughs of New York seemed to know when or where he'd been born. It seemed almost fitting: Aurelio was dead, and our final day of the surveillance was over. Two closures. One sad, the other nothing short of absurd.

I made what I thought would be my last trip to the Jones Beach Hotel, at Santini's request. He met me there in the lobby late in the afternoon, handed over the balance of my fee, and departed. He didn't even waste time on small talk. I could see by his manner that he was not happy the surveillance had ended, but he'd given his word, and, oddly enough, he was keeping it. As I drove back to Bensonhurst, I wondered if the imagined threat was in fact as real as he'd said it was, if I would read about his murder some morning in the *Daily News*. It wouldn't bother me much if one of the people he'd suspected finally did kill him, but if it did happen, there would always be doubts in my mind that I could have done the job better, that I could have prevented the killing somehow. He'd hired me not only as a spy, but also as a bodyguard of sorts, and there is no greater failure for a bodyguard than seeing harm come to the person who hired you.

The office was quiet for a week afterward, so quiet that I gave Arnie some well-deserved time off. I'd paid him and my temporary operatives, more than seventeen hundred dollars each. Pretty substantial wages for a worthless and futile effort, now mercifully concluded. I thought that Viper would leave immediately for parts unknown, but for some reason he was staying close. Watusi insisted that he was waiting for his family to arrive, by Greyhound bus, from Los Angeles, but I had my doubts. I'd heard nothing more from Santini, and nothing from Nick DeMassio. It was as if the whole thing hadn't happened. And so I didn't expect the phone call I got from Arnie late that Monday night at home.

"He's dead!" Arnie shouted frantically into the handset, his voice thick with fear and fury. "Dead!"

"Santini?"

"No. *Charlie*. My buddy Charlie. He's fuckin' dead!"

My mind went blank for a moment. "*Who's* dead?"

"Jesus, Eddie! *Charlie.* My buddy from the Corps. The guy who was trailin' that chauffeur for you. He's dead. Shot dead!"

"Where?"

"Pay phone, corner of Flatbush and Beverly in Flatlands, near the Loew's Kings. A couple of blocks from his place on Avenue H. I'm out here now with the cops. Both our names were in Charlie's address book, so the cops say they wanna talk to both of us."

"Where are you calling from?" I asked.

"A bar just down the street. They wouldn't let me use the phone where Charlie got shot. How soon can you get over here?"

I made it in less than half an hour, running a couple of stoplights in the process. Three black-and-whites were at the scene, red lights flashing. Beyond them were the coroner's wagon and two unmarked cars that probably belonged to forensics and a pair of detective-lieutenants. The 63rd Precinct patrolled this part of Brooklyn. I didn't know anybody at the 63rd, so I decided to practice my best behavior. I was making enemies faster than I was making friends these days among New York's Finest, so it paid to be polite at the very least.

The body was half-in, half-out of the phone booth. His darkening blood was pooled under him. He lay face down with his right arm extended, as if he'd been reaching for the dial when the three bullets struck him in the back. Arnie was talking to one of the detectives. He stopped when he saw me, motioned me to come closer, and pointed at the detective.

"Wilkinson, detective-lieutenant, 63rd," said the man. "You're Lombardi?"

I nodded.

"So, this man, the deceased, was working for you?"

"For a short stretch. Surveillance job," I said. "Nothing out of the ordinary."

"Any reason you know why somebody would want him dead?"

"None that I know of."

"Just a surveillance job, you say?"

"That's all it was."

"Who was he following?"

"Just a guy. Domestic matter." There was no point in delving into Jimmy Santini's assassination fantasies, or the fact that Charlie had been tailing Santini's chauffeur for me. There'd be time later to tell the cop, if it became necessary. I knew already that Arnie would have kept silent about the Santini connection. The detective turned his attention back to him.

"Enemies?" he asked.

"Didn't have any," Arnie answered. "No family to speak of, either. Korean War vet like me. Lived over the Rand Cleaners on Avenue H. Quiet guy. Nice guy. Goddamn shame."

"Well, nobody saw it," said the cop. "But people in the apartments, they heard the gunshots. Looks like he tried to make a call. Phone's off the hook, so he might have dialed a number before he took the bullets, or maybe not. We'll check it out with the phone company. Anything else you might want to tell us?"

Arnie's teeth were gritted, so I knew he wasn't up for an answer. I kept silent.

"Okay," the detective said. "If you can give us any more help, any at all, we'd appreciate it."

"Any ideas of your own?" I asked the cop. Arnie was already walking back to his car.

"Doesn't look like a random killing to me. Doesn't look like street murder. The wallet still has money in it. And killing him here on the main drag, that's not how it's done. Not by the people who make this kind of thing their business."

"And he was trying to call somebody," I said absently.

"You, maybe?"

Arnie was waiting next to his car, smoking a cigarette. He hadn't had enough time to cool off yet, so I tried to give him some before I said anything. But Arnie wasn't going to wait. Not for either of us.

"I'm gonna get the sonofabitch who did this," he said through snarling lips. "I swear to God, Eddie. I'm gonna find the sonofabitch and kill him."

"You need a drink, maybe," I said. "We both need one. We can go to that bar down the street, talk for a while, maybe."

"Gonna get him."

"Sure. I know. Then again, maybe the bar's not such a good idea. Why don't you just go home? Have a beer or two where the booze won't do you any harm. Get some sleep. We can talk in the morning."

"Yeah, sure," he said, hollow-voiced. "Talk in the morning."

"You'll feel better."

"Sure, sure."

"A little sleep, that's all."

"Yeah. Sure."

"I'm sorry this happened, Arnie."

"Sure, sure."

"Damn thing is, the chauffeur was the least likely suspect on the list. No criminal record, no mob connections. Keeping tabs on him should've been a walk in the park. But now he's dead, and so's your buddy. There's something wrong there."

"Yeah," said Arnie, holding back tears. "Somethin's wrong."

"Maybe it's unconnected," I said. "Maybe it *was* just a street crime. Wrong place, wrong time. But who was he trying to call?" I gave Arnie a brotherly look. "You sure you're okay, partner?" I asked, but he didn't answer, so I asked again. He glared at me for a moment, then got into his car and started the motor.

"No," Arnie said. "I'm not," and he drove away.

16

Arnie was in the office when I arrived at eight the next morning. Usually I'd find him sitting behind my desk with his feet up in a pose of perfect nonchalance, but not this time. He stood at the bank of windows looking out onto 18th Avenue. He didn't turn when I walked in.

I sat at my desk and waited for him.

"You okay?" I asked.

"You already know the answer to that one," he said, without turning.

"All right," I said. "What's your beef?"

When he did turn, slowly, deliberately, he showed me a look I'd seen in him only once or twice before: a look of pure murder.

"This Santini business," he said in a low growl of a voice. "It's not over."

"Care to explain?" I said.

"Charlie."

"I told you I was sorry about that."

"He killed him. Had him killed."

"Who?"

"Santini. Who else?"

"You think *Santini* had Charlie killed?"

"I don't know. Maybe. Probably."

"And if he didn't?"

"I don't know. I just know this thing's not over."

I got out of my chair so quickly that it should have squeaked. It didn't. "Oh, but it *is*, partner. You just ask my wife."

"I'm serious, Eddie," he said, firmly but without his usual petulance. "Charlie's murder, it's tied to Santini somehow. I know it is."

I sat down again. "All right," I said as calmly as I could manage. "I'm waiting for your explanation."

"I don't have one."

"You don't *have* one?"

"I just *know*."

"Oh, for Chrissake, Arnie. First Santini goes goofy on me, and now you? You want to tell me what Ouija board you're getting all your ideas from? You've got no proof at all it was Santini. Not even a suspicion of proof."

"There's no other way, Eddie. No other way it happens if Charlie wasn't on the case. The case ain't closed. Not for me, anyway."

"So, what do I do? Call up Liam and Watusi and Viper and tell them we're still working on the case, except that they're not going to get paid this time?"

"No. It's none of their business. It's my business, and, I'm hopin' you'll make it your business, too. Charlie, he was workin' for us, for Lombardi Investigations. We owe him."

"Arnie..."

"We got no new cases. What else would we do but sit in the office?"

"But if we *do* get one..."

"Then we stop, officially. Then it's my case, on my own time."

I leaned back in my chair, again expecting to hear it squeak. It was a comforting sound in difficult moments like this one. When it didn't make a sound, comforting or otherwise, I looked at Arnie. There was a tight but slowly widening smile on his face, the first smile he'd shown in some time.

"I oiled the sonofabitch," he said. "Now, about this Santini business. Just hear me out. How many suspects we got left?"

"Real suspects? Santini's suspects? Well, the Barracuda Brothers have come clean, and the chauffeur's dead, so that leaves four. And only two of those have what might roughly be called motives: the wife and the lawyer. Now, the wife, she knows he's been cheating on her, but she's getting a divorce, and it's almost final, so Watusi thinks she's got no reason to murder her husband. It would tie up the settlement, and I'm sure it's a very nice settlement."

"And the lawyer?"

"The lawyer's a homosexual. He doesn't seem to care who knows it, but Santini tries to embarrass the guy every chance he gets. Could be something there. Maybe the lawyer has payback in mind for all the embarrassment he's been swallowing from Santini and the Barracuda Brothers. Of course, if he kills Santini, he's lost his only client. Not that he couldn't pick up another."

"What about the daughter and her shrink?"

"*You're* the one who was following the daughter. Did she do anything weird that last week?"

"Well, not weird, but...one thing."

"Which is?"

"Last day of that last week before we quit, I followed her to a printer's out in Brownsville. Dial Printing. It's on Sutter Avenue."

"And?"

"She went into the print shop, came out maybe fifteen minutes later, and drove back to Gravesend."

"And?"

"Nothin' wrong with that, I suppose, but there's plenty of printers' shops in her own neighborhood. One of em's only a couple of blocks away from Santini's estate. Why would she want to go all the way out to Brownsville to have some printin' done?"

"Maybe they're the best printer in the Borough. Or the planet. How would I know?"

"The place is a *dump*, Eddie. And the neighborhood's not exactly where white-gloved little Italian princesses would want to drive their pink T-Birds if they didn't have to. And then there's the little lady's very expensive shrink."

"Rothberg?"

"I know he was your big spook's guy to watch, but maybe there's somethin' goin' on there."

"Like what?"

"Well, she went to see him a couple of times last week. I *tailed* her there a couple o' times, anyway. But does anybody even know why she goes there, why she needs to see a shrink? I mean, what's her problem?"

"Being Jimmy Santini's daughter is no doubt a contributing factor. Other than that, there's no way to know. The psychiatrist is certainly not going to tell us. And there's nothing nefarious about seeing one."

Arnie squinted at me.

"'Nefarious,'" I said. "It means evil, immoral, reprehensible."

"Reprehensible?"

"Never mind. Anyway, none of this guessing will get us anywhere. If you've got a practical suggestion that might lead us somewhere, spill it."

"Okay. First off, I wouldn't bother with the lawyer. I mean, if the Brothers are tailin' him, that oughta be enough. Anyway, I don't figure him to be the murderin' type. Then again, he might just hire somebody to do the job, but I don't think so. Me, I'd keep up the surveillance on the wife."

"And your reasons?"

"Don't really have any. I just got a feelin' about her."

"Jesus," I said, my shoulders sagging. "Am I the only one here who isn't a fucking psychic?"

"I guess not. Are you game?"

"Everything else about this case has been screwy," I said. "So, if that's what you want to do..."

"That's what I want. Maybe nothin' will happen. Maybe we'll strike out on both Charlie's killer and whoever's still gunning for Santini, if anybody is. But we gotta try."

"It's your call," I said. "What's the plan?"

"Eight hour shifts. You take the days, and I'll take the nights. We follow the wife."

"That still makes eight hours we can't cover," I said.

"Then I'll take those, too."

"Seven days a *week*?" I said, offering a skeptical look. "Didn't we just get past that kind of craziness?"

"I'll do it," he said, stiffening, scowling harder.

"And Liam? And Watusi?"

"Unless they wanna work for no pay, they're out. This isn't their fight."

"And if we get new business?"

"Then *you're* out."

"Okay. How long?"

"Until we get new business."

"And if I need you?"

He gave me the kind of cock-sure grin I'd seen only on one other face: my *goombah* Frankie DeFilippo. "There's twenty-four hours in a day, Eddie," he said. "And I only owe you eight of 'em."

"All right."

"The wife, she's all yours until six o'clock tonight. I'll keep track of her after that. And if nothin' pans out in a couple o' days, we start tailin' the daughter. Okay?"

"And why the daughter?"

"On account of that out-of–the-way print shop in Brownsville, and because she'd be the only suspect left."

"And if *she* doesn't pan out?"

"Then, like I said, I'm on my own time. Charlie's murderer. I'm gonna find him, and you can just bet on it."

I smiled. "I wouldn't bet on anything else, partner."

17

It was another bust following Santini's wife that morning and afternoon. Taking the same black Pontiac that Santini used to drive me to the Jones Beach Hotel, she went to a beauty parlor on Ocean Avenue, met two fashionably dressed women for lunch at Lundy's in Sheepshead Bay, and concluded her travels at the fine counters of Abraham & Strauss on Fulton Street. I met Arnie back at the office at six, apprised him of the day's non-events, and went home to my wife and children.

I finished reading *The Wind in the Willows* with Amanda and Mary, and then Laura and I settled in on the living room couch with a bottle of *strega* and two glasses of her best crystal. I had a fire going, and Frank Sinatra was singing "Young at Heart" on the phonograph. Domesticity at its best, and one of the sure-fire remedies for a troubled marriage.

"Shouldn't we do this every night?" I asked finally. She was so close to me that I wondered if we could ever be separate people again. As if our bodies had been fused together by the magic of the wine and the music and the firelight. Her eyes sparkled in it, and I felt some stirrings down below my belt. To repress the impulse, I tried reciting the names of the saints, alphabetically, inside my head.

"You were saying," she asked, dreamy eyed.

"Oh, nothing. I meant the music. It would be nice if we listened to music every night."

"To get us in the mood?"

"Mood? For what?"

"For more of this."

"I'm right with you on that one," I said.

"I'm glad the Santini business is over with," she said. She looked at me warmly, but I couldn't speak. And when I turned my eyes away, she knew.

"It's not quite over," I said before she could ask, and I explained about Arnie's pal Charlie.

"Oh, Eddie, no..."

"I don't expect a whole lot from it, Laura, and it won't last for long, I promise. It's just to give Arnie a way to deal with everything. He's the one who brought Charlie into the operation, and he'll sulk himself into a major bender or worse if I don't let him loose. I owe him that much. And he's so damn sure that he's right, even if he doesn't know why."

"Like your Mr. Santini was right?"

"That's past history, Laura."

"Is it?"

"The funny thing is, they're *both* sure. And odd things *have* been happening. I don't know what to think at this point."

"But your job's over."

"Officially, yes. And Santini's still alive."

"Maybe they share the same crystal ball," she said, curling up closer to me, smiling coyly. "Arnie and Santini, I mean. Maybe you should get one yourself."

"And what exactly would I do with it: predict murders that weren't ever going to happen?"

"I was thinking of more practical domestic uses. Like, which handsome, well-heeled gentlemen are waiting in the future for our two little girls. Like, whether Amanda will go to Harvard University someday. Or Yale. She's smart as a whip, you know."

"And Mary?"

"We won't need a crystal ball for Mary. She's only two, but she already knows her numbers and letters. And she's a pure charmer. The boys will simply swarm around her, and she'll break the heart of every boy she meets, until the right one comes along. *Very* selective she is, and very determined."

"You're not telling me what I don't know," I said.

"You can still know more."

"Uh oh. Am I getting the You-Need-to-Be-More-of-a-Homebody talk again?"

"Not in so many words."
"It'll be over soon," I said.
"That's what you said last time."

I got up early the next morning, before the sun had risen. Laura and the girls were still asleep, and I didn't want to make a lot of noise in the kitchen, so I walked over to the office on 18th Avenue and made fresh coffee on the hotplate. Arnie wasn't due to report until six o'clock that evening, so I had time to think about our conversation from the day before. Despite his certainty that Santini's wife was our prime suspect, I wasn't comfortable with the idea. His mention of Maria Santini and the out-of-the-way print shop was what got me thinking. It was just another anomaly without an explanation, innocent enough, probably; but I couldn't get the idea out of my mind. So I gassed up the Chrysler wagon at the Texaco and drove to Brownsville. I had the time, and it wouldn't hurt to check out the place and get some background on the owner. Arnie was right about it not being the best neighborhood for a white-gloved Italian princess in a T-Bird. A corner candy store at Lavonia and Saratoga Avenues had once been the headquarters for Murder, Incorporated. The neighborhood hadn't improved much since, even though Murder, Inc. was now just a footnote in its dark history.

Arnie hadn't been wrong about it being a dump, either. The canvas awning that hung over the storefront was torn and stained, and the plate glass window had been blacked out with old newsprint. So, why *would* she come here if she could have gone to places closer to home and safer? Was the printing quality that good? Or the price? And what did price matter to her, a Mafia kingpin's hopelessly spoiled daughter? It made me think a moment back to Santini's original plans for her: a convent where she could prepare herself to be a Bride of Christ. I knew why it hadn't happened, of course, but a good many years had passed since that non-event, and there was no reason to tie it in with this current unpleasantness.

Or was there?

A buxom middle-aged woman in a print dress greeted me at the counter when I went inside. The space was tight, low ceilinged, and the lighting was minimal. Everything smelled of machine oil and printer's ink.

"Good morning," I said. "My name's Lombardi. Thomas Lombardi. My niece, Maria Santini, sent me to pick up her order, if it's ready."

"Santini, you said?" she asked pleasantly.

"Yes."

"Let me check and see," she said, and disappeared through a narrow doorway that led to the printing room. I heard presses running. The smell of printer's ink and machine oil increased, then faded when the door closed again behind her. When she returned, she offered a small scowl. "That's a special order," she said, "and it's not ready yet. Did Miss Santini tell you it was?"

"Well, no, actually. But I was in the neighborhood, and I thought if it was ready, I could pick it up for her."

"I'm sorry," she said. "But it's a special order, and she is the only person with the authority to pick it up."

I moved closer and leaned over the counter toward her. I held out a fiver, smiled, and then placed it on the counter. "Here's the thing," I said. "Some of us relatives, we think maybe she's planning some kind of a surprise. This special order that you're filling, would you happen to know if it's a wedding announcement? Could you show me?"

"I've already told you, sir," she said, pushing back the bribe with a stiff arm. "Only Miss Santini is authorized to pick up the order. I'm very sorry."

I pushed the fiver back in her direction. "For your trouble," I said, and left the shop.

It was just after noon when I arrived back in Bensonhurst. Rather than go home or stop for a quick lunch at the Bella Italia Luncheonette, I drove to the Santini estate in Gravesend and waited, hoping that the soon-not-to-be Mrs. James Santini hadn't done anything incriminating while I was following my latest hunches in Brownsville. Maybe Arnie *was* right about her. Maybe this time she'd roll past those imposing cast-iron gates and lead me finally to some answers. Anyway, I had nothing better to do. I needed a quick follow-up on the trip to Dial Printing, but there was nobody to do it. Aurelio would have been perfect for the job, but he was with the angels now. Or the devils. I needed a new snitch, but I wasn't sure where to start looking. Maybe the guy that Aurelio had called a rummy.

Just after one o'clock, Mrs. Santini drove the black Pontiac to the Williamsburg Savings Bank on Hanson Place. It was more than just a bank –– the forty-two-floor building had a number of other offices inside –– but it was safe to say that she was probably making deposits or withdrawals. I assumed that she had her own accounts, and once the divorce was final, she'd have a lot more in those accounts. She drove from there to Albemarle Road. I had to check the address from my notes, but there was no question: she was paying a call on Dr. Meyer Rothberg, Maria Santini's psychiatrist. Paying an overdue bill, perhaps? Discussing the effect her upcoming divorce would have on her already troubled stepdaughter? Or was it another kind of visit? My naturally suspicious mind was in overdrive.

She drove back to the Santini estate less than an hour later, and I followed. She went exactly nowhere for the rest of the day. When Arnie drove up at six to take the night shift, I returned to the office. Two phone calls had been left with my answering service. The first was the office supply company again, inquiring if I needed more business envelopes or stationery. The second was Nick DeMassio. So I called.

"Been talking with Mike French, the captain over at the 63rd," he said, matter-of-factly. "Heard about your operative who got shot in the phone booth. Mike says to tell you that if your guy was tryin' to call somebody, the call never went through."

"The phone was off the hook," I said.

"Yeah, but apparently he didn't have time to place a call. That's all they know over at the 63rd. Anything *you* want to tell me about the guy?"

"He'd been keeping an eye on Santini's chauffeur."

"The one that burned up in the fire?"

"That's one way to put it," I said.

"Is there another way?"

"Maybe."

"You got other ideas?"

"Not at the moment, Nick. But I've got questions."

"Like?"

"Like if somebody was going to kill the guy and burn him up, why bash his skull in like that? For that matter, why burn him up at all?"

"Lot of anger there."

"Maybe too much," I said.

"Meaning?"

"The ax and all. It's overkill."

"Like I said. Lot of anger. Heat of the moment, no pun intended. You still think Santini iced him?"

"I don't know who iced him. Or who killed my operative. Or why."

"Need a motive, huh?"

"Something like that, especially if Santini wasn't the one who had him iced."

"It wasn't Jimmy Santini in the alley, if that's what you're thinkin'," said DeMassio. "Wrong body type, from what the witnesses saw. That guy was tall and slender, and Santini's built like an earthmover. Besides, he wouldn't stoop to doin' it himself."

"Well, somebody wanted that chauffeur deader than dead."

"And he got what he wanted."

"Yeah," I said, and sighed.

"Well, anyway, keep in touch," said Nick, which meant that he was about to hang up on me.

"Hold on," I said. "Wait a sec."

118

"Yeah?"

"Are we friends enough now for me to ask a favor?"

"I didn't know we were friends at all," he said. I could almost see his brow furrowing.

"Well, are we?"

"Maybe. It depends."

"On what?"

"On whether you plan to become my personal hemorrhoid again. I could do without that."

"No, and that's a promise," I said.

"Okay. What you wanna know?"

"There's a printing shop, Dial Printing, over in Brownsville. Can you find out if it's legit for me?"

"Same case?"

"Only one I've got at the moment."

"So why can't you find out for yourself? Too busy for the small stuff?"

"Truth is, I lost my snitch."

"Rodriguez?"

"You knew him?"

"Sure. Us cops, we know all the snitches. Part of the job. Unless you think we get all our information from the newspapers and the public library."

"Did he ever work for you?"

He laughed. "How do you think I've kept track of *you* all these years?"

"Aurelio?"

"Among others."

"Double agent," I said, and smiled. "Son of a bitch."

"And?"

"Just thinking out loud, that's all."

"Okay. For what it's worth, I'll check the place out," he said. And he hung up.

"Son of a bitch," I said again, for my own ears.

18

On the third day of our surveillance, on my suggestion, Arnie and I changed our stakeout plan and followed Maria Santini and her pink T-Bird. I'd take her daytime wanderings, and Arnie would follow her each evening. She offered no surprises during the first day of my watch: a luncheon engagement at 21 Club on 52nd Street in Midtown, a trip to a car wash on Ocean Parkway, and an hour and a half at Saks Fifth Avenue. I was hoping that she'd make another trip to the print shop out in Brownsville, but she disappointed me, driving back home an hour before my watch was over and staying there. When Arnie relieved me at six o'clock, I told him, belatedly, about my trip to Dial Printing, Mrs. Santini's visit to Dr. Rothberg's, and my phone call from Captain DeMassio. I went back to the office to check with my answering service before going home, but there had been no calls. Not even from the office supply company.

And then the phone rang. It was Liam O'Rourke.

"There once was an Eye-talian bloke
Whose leads always went up in smoke..."

"And to what do I owe this honor?" I said, showing some of Arnie's petulance.

"Business is slack, Eddie lad. There's been no fookin' work to speak of."

"And so?"

"You might be rememberin', lad, that you gave me a wee job to do before you gave us all the fookin' ax on that Santini business."

"And your fucking pay," I countered. "Which wasn't all that insignificant, if you remember."

"Well, here's the thing, lad. You remember our late lamented limo driver? One Harry Appolino?"

"I do."

"You were wantin' me to find out who his family was, and where they might be found among these blessed Five Boroughs."

"And?"

"Plenty of Appolinos in the phone books. Not an easy job, mind you. Hard work and then some."

"And?"

"Truth be told, lad, I found them. But they're not here in Brooklyn. Queens, that's where they are. Jackson Heights, to be exact, off Astoria Boulevard, near the airport. Nice little two-family on 92nd Street."

"And you've talked to them?"

"Well, kind of subtle-like. Asked the neighbors, mostly. The dear *pater*, his name's Tomaso. Steamfitter. Big burly chap. The *mater*, Dolores, she's strictly a homebody. Spends her time makin' *manicotti* and puttin' up peach preserves. Poor Harry, he was their only kid."

"That's it?"

"Patience, lad, patience. I'm buildin' up to me generous cash bonus, don't you know."

"And?"

"The mother. She's the key to it." He paused for effect, and let it linger.

"I'm still listening."

"Her maiden name was Gabriano. Dolores Gabriano. Does the name ring a bell, Eddie lad?"

He knew that it would. Still, I decided to bust his balls for trying to bust mine. "Gabriano? Sure. Joe Gabriano. He's a realtor in Flatbush. Ran into him on the last Jack Janus case."

"*Rocco* Gabriano, Eddie lad. And he was no fookin' realtor from Flatbush or anyplace else. He was one of Jimmy Santini's number one boys before he..."

"Yes, I know," I said.

"Well, this Harry Appolino's mom, her older brother is our Rocco's dear *pater*, which made Rocco Gabriano our late Harry's older cousin. Now, knowin' the tragic history of all these folks, and rememberin' the fact that our dear, late Rocco was the one that kept sweet Maria out of the convent, maybe Santini had a good reason for knockin' off the young cousin. You think maybe?"

I was listening, but I didn't have an answer. Instead of clearing the muddy water I was swimming in, Liam had only stirred the thickening mud a little more.

"Well?" he asked, nearly matching my own petulance.

"That was a long time ago," I said finally.

"There's no fookin' statute o' limitations on revenge, lad."

"Your point being?"

"The kid, he wants to get back at Santini for killin' his dear cousin Rocco and dumpin' him in Gravesend Bay with his pecker stuck in his throat. So, he finds a way to get himself the job as Santini's limo driver. Now, he's ready to do the dirty deed straightaway; but then Santini finds him out somehow, cooks up that crazy murder plot, suckers you in to make it all official, and has the kid killed and burned to toast before the kid can do the bleedin' same to him."

"Santini wouldn't need me as protection," I said. "He'd just do it."

"Truth be told, lad. Truth be told. Now, I don't know how –- or even if -- this piece fits in with the rest of the bleedin' puzzle, but..."

"Meaning, if anybody else is going to get whacked?"

"Don't know, lad. All I'm sayin' is, if you want to know why poor Harry Appolino's dead, there's your fookin' reason. It all goes back to Rocco."

"I hung dear Rocco out a fourth-floor window once," I said in a moment of sweet reminiscence. "Did you know that? It was at a police station. The captain's name was Halsman, if I remember correctly. Real crooked cop. Scared the shit out of him."

"Halsman?"

"No. Rocco. I almost let the bastard drop, too. Should have, probably. Not that it would have made any difference. It was your photos of him and the daughter that sealed his fate with Jimmy

Santini. That's why Santini thinks that we're such pals, because I told him about Rocco and his daughter."

"Aye. So it was."

"In that alley outside the Steeplechase Bar at Coney."

"And you delivered the fatal message, lad. Where was it, again?"

"Ebbets Field," I said. "A long time ago."

"No statute o' limitations, Eddie lad."

"True enough."

"So, how much of a big, fat bonus do I get for me fine fookin' work, for crackin' this case wide open?"

I was hoping he wouldn't catch the irony in my voice when I answered. "How about I buy you Santini's modest little palace in Gravesend, after he moves on to Sing Sing?"

"I'll be holdin' you to that promise, lad," he said, and hung up on me.

I stayed in the office for a while before going home. It made sense, the way Liam had explained it, but I couldn't shake the feeling that there was something else still churning in the mix, something I *felt* more than knew. Something that fit the facts in a different way. Something that *changed* the facts as everybody understood them, or *thought* they understood them. The facts all right, but ass backwards and twisted, like looking at them in a funhouse mirror. Like Alice and her looking glass. I re-read the case file from '47 on Rocco, but it didn't clear things up any. Rocco and Maria Santini had been just part of a larger puzzle that I'd been trying to put together at the time. And their secret tryst had been incidental to that case at best.

And now, almost thirteen years later, was it somehow rearing up again? What *were* the facts, anyway?

Laura had my late dinner waiting for me. Amanda and Mary were waiting in their bedroom for the new story I was going to read them: *Anne of Green Gables*. But then Arnie called in a frantic voice and told me -- ordered me -- to meet him at the office. I tried twice to make him wait until morning, but he wouldn't have it.

Laura shamed me with a look as I left the house, and both girls started crying.

"This better be good," I said when I met Arnie outside the office. The Bella Italia Luncheonette on the ground floor was just closing. Arnie was standing beside his car, in a manner of speaking, since his arms and legs were both in a state of extreme agitation. I hadn't seen him this jacked up in a while, and so I added with a sly grin, "You playing around with that marijuana again?"

"Get in the car," he said, so I did. We drove east. I waited for him to calm down. He didn't.

"I'm waiting, Arnie," I said bluntly. "My wife is pissed, and my two girls are crying. This damn well better be good."

"Okay, okay," he said. "Here's the deal. I waited outside Santini's gate like I always do, and around seven, the T-Bird pulls out, so I follow it. To Flatlands, as it turns out, to a bar just off Flatbush Avenue. She parks the T-Bird, and she goes inside."

"And what time is this again?"

"Around seven-thirty, by the time she got there. And she went *straight there.* No other stops."

"What's the name of the bar?"

"The Crazy Horse. It's on Duryea Place."

"And?" I said.

"I park about a block away, and I wait to see what happens. After about a half-hour, she comes out, she puts on those damn prissy driving gloves, and she goes back home. Again, no stops."

"So, she went to a bar, okay. Nothing special there."

Arnie pulled the car suddenly to the curb. "Eddie, the *bar* -- the fuckin' *bar* -- it's right around the corner from the Loew's Kings. It's a fuckin' *block away* from the phone booth at Flatbush and Beverly where Charlie got gunned down. You just turn the corner from Duryea onto Flatbush Avenue, and you can *see* the fuckin' phone booth."

He showed me again when we arrived outside the bar, walking excitedly to the corner, pointing past the marquee of the Loew's Kings, pointing at the public phone on the next corner.

"And don't fuckin' tell me it's a coincidence," he said.

I gave him a long look, and a longer moment for him to regain his composure. "No," I said finally. "I don't imagine that it is. Have you got a picture of Charlie with you?"

"The cops, they already asked. They showed it around. At the Loew's, at the bar, at anyplace that was open that time o' night. The bartender said the crowd was large and noisy. There was a prizefight going on the television. If Charlie was in there, he was lost in the crowd. And she walked into that same bar. Tonight."

"Her reason?"

"To meet somebody."

"An assassin?"

"Somebody. No way to know. And no way to know why she made that trip out to the printer in Brownsville."

"I've got Captain DeMassio working on that, if you can believe it. And then there's what Liam told me just a couple of hours ago." I explained it to him.

"You think Santini and the daughter are in it together?"

"Maybe. Or maybe not. You can't convict her on a conspiracy charge just because she goes to an out-of-the-way printer or because she goes to an out-of-the-way bar. No judge would even listen to a case that lame."

"You just agreed it wasn't a coincidence."

"Well, and then just maybe it was. How the hell do I know what she was doing there, or why?"

"Let me stay on this a while," he said. "I could hang out at The Crazy Horse for a couple of nights, just to see if she comes back, or I could just ask around, see if anybody remembers her and whoever she was meetin'."

"Another long shot," I said.

"That's all we've been doin' lately is long shots, for Chrissake."

"Okay, you could try that, but you'd stick out like a sore thumb and come across like a cop. If you ask me, she's made her one trip out here for whatever reason, and she probably won't make another. But we'll keep a closer eye on her, wherever she does go."

"It's no coincidence," Arnie insisted when we arrived back at the car.

"We'll see. Anyway, it's still your call."

"I told you," he said again. "I told you Charlie's killin' had somethin' to do with Santini."

"Not until we can prove it, partner. We've got the same suspects, minus one, and a few unconfirmed suspicions about them. And that's *all* we've got."

"Until we get more," he said.

"Yeah. Until then. We're still looking for miracles."

"Well, they *happen*, don't they?"

"No often enough."

19

I thought Laura might lock me out of the house by the time I got home, but she'd mellowed some. Not enough for real cordiality, and light years away from wifely affection, but good enough for the moment. I finally ate my cold supper around midnight. And there was still some *strega* left when we sat in front of an even colder fireplace at one in the morning.

"I read the girls the first chapter of the new book," she said. "I was informed, and in no uncertain terms, that you read to them better than I do. Amanda went so far as to suggest that you read a practice story to me so I could see how it's done."

"You're not jealous, are you?"

"No, but I am curious."

"They see me less, and so they appreciate me more," I said, almost deadpan.

"Is that it?"

"No. It's just that they're used to me reading to them. If I ever tried to make their breakfast, finicky as they both are, they'd probably throw it back in my face."

"I was thinking again about the crystal ball thing," she said softly, a small gleam in her eyes.

"About Amanda and Harvard?"

"No, about you. I thought, wouldn't it be nice if you could tell parents where their runaway teenagers had gone, or who'd robbed the corner supermarket, all without leaving the house?"

"Is there a sale at F.A.O. Schwarz? They probably sell that kind of stuff."

"I'd buy one tomorrow, if it would keep you home more."

"It's almost over," I said.

"'Almost' is a big word, Eddie. Are we talking about the evening, the current case, or your career?"

"Will you settle for two out of three?" I asked, and she got up and went to bed.

The plan was still to keep our eyes on Maria and her travels in the pink T-Bird, so I parked the Chrysler once again outside the Santini estate at eight the next morning and waited. She drove first to Dr. Rothberg's home on Albemarle Road, stayed the standard fifty minutes, and then drove to Brownsville. Dial Printing. She left after only a few minutes, gassed up the T-Bird at a Sunoco station on Shore parkway, and hit the road again, cruising languidly around the marshes and bogs in Canarsie and Jamaica Bay. On her way back, she even took a detour onto Flatbush Avenue in Flatlands, driving past the Loew's Kings, past Duryea Place and The Crazy Horse Bar, past the phone booth at Flatbush and Beverly, and all of it without stopping. Arnie wouldn't like hearing that. It didn't jibe with his theories. As far as I was concerned, we still had four suspects, or we had or none at all. Liam's argument about Santini, Rocco Gabriano, and Harry Appolino had gained some weight in my mind, but it didn't connect up with anything else. By the time I'd followed the pink T-Bird home at five that afternoon, I wasn't sure of anything.

I decided to shift gears again and follow Santini's lawyer for a while. I'd fill Arnie in on the change in plan when he came to the office at six. He'd been itching to check out Julius' anyway. But Arnie didn't report in for his shift. I called his apartment, but he wasn't there. I thought about driving to Santini's estate to see if he was parked outside, but I figured he knew what he was doing, wherever he was. So I closed up the office and went home.

I went in earlier than usual the next morning. I checked my answering service, but Arnie hadn't called. I spent some time on the files, brewed some A&P Bokar on the hotplate, and waited for the phone to ring. Three cups of coffee later it did, but it wasn't Arnie on the line. It was Nick DeMassio.

"You wanted to know about Dial Printing in Brownsville?" he asked.

"I did," I said.

"Looks legitimate. A little run down, maybe, but no red flags are comin' up. At least, no current investigations that involve the place."

"That's what you said about that duck farm on the Island," I said. "The one that was really just a big cemetery for the Mob."

"Okay, okay. So, we missed on that one. I'm just tellin' you, the printer looks to be legit. Just a little on the seedy side, that's all. The building's owned by a guy named Rothberg."

"*Meyer* Rothberg? The psychiatrist?"

"Yeah. You know him?"

I explained. It was quiet at DeMassio's end for a long moment, and then he said, almost contritely, "We'll look a little deeper, then," before hanging up.

I decided to shift gears again. Suddenly, it was Rothberg's turn.

I waited another ten futile minutes to hear from Arnie, and when he didn't show or call, I drove to Albemarle Road. Rothberg stayed at his office all that morning and into early afternoon. He had a steady stream of clients coming and going. The usual fifty-minute sessions; nothing outside the ordinary. Santini's wife didn't show, but his daughter arrived just after two and stayed for the usual time. That surprised me, because she'd just been there the day before. Breaking my own rules of engagement, I decided to follow her when she drove away. She went east again, along the Shore Parkway. There were several access roads, mostly packed dirt and gravel, that led to the shore, but I decided not to follow her in. It was an isolated place at this time of day. Even the fly fishermen had gone home. She re-emerged about ten minutes later and drove to the wetlands around Floyd Bennett Field, taking yet another narrow access road that ended at Jamaica Bay. Again, I didn't follow, and again the pink T-Bird re-emerged, mud-spattered. It turned west onto Shore Parkway again, first to a car wash in Flatlands, and then home. I drove back to Rothberg's place on Albemarle Road, lingered another half hour there, and then returned to the office, where Arnie was waiting.

"Where the hell have you been?" he asked.

"I might ask you the same thing," I said, scowling.

"I went AWOL on you last night," he said without apology. "Back to that bar in Flatlands. Back to where Charlie got shot. I showed his picture around. I know, I know. You told me not to. Anyway, nobody recognized him. He wasn't a regular. There were even some guys in there last night who were there the night he got killed, but all they knew was that they heard shots outside, and later the cops arrived. So, it was a big fuckin' waste of time. If you wanna chew me out, just go ahead."

Arnie's unreliability was showing again, but this wasn't the best time to call him on it, so I let it pass. "I went AWOL myself today," I said, and explained about Meyer Rothberg and following the T-Bird out to the marshes.

"Didn't figure the princess for a nature lover," said Arnie. "You think she maybe met somebody out there?"

"Beats me," I said. "I doubt she's into fly fishing."

"You think maybe she's just fuckin' with us? Like maybe she knows we've been followin' her and she's decided to lead us everyplace and no place?"

"Could be. I don't know."

"And what about this Rothberg guy? Do we keep an eye on *him* now?"

I explained about Nick DeMassio's call.

"The printer again. Coincidence?"

"DeMassio said he'd look into it a little deeper, but you know what that means."

"Too bad that crazy spic died on you, Eddie. You need another snitch."

"I might have one," I said. "His name's Enrico Rosario."

"Come again?"

"He's a snitch, like Aurelio. Aurelio said he was a rummy, which I guess means he's unreliable. Of course, Aurelio was a hopeless alcoholic himself, but he was as reliable as wind in a hurricane."

"You could look this guy up."

"I could, indeed."

"And me?"

"Stick with Rothberg. For tonight, anyway."

There were several Enrico Rosarios in the phone books of the Five Boroughs, so I started dialing. The third one I called was the one I wanted. He lived on Lafayette Avenue near Fort Greene Park.

"So, who the hell are you?" he asked in a gruff, Hispanic voice. Almost an echo of Aurelio, but a full octave deeper. I heard the low rumble of street traffic in the background.

"I'm a friend of Aurelio's," I said.

He laughed. "Aurelio, he didn't *have* no friends, except for that J.T.S. Brown shit. He wasn't *my* fuckin' friend."

"Aurelio told me you were a guy I should see," I added. "For tips and information of a particular variety."

"That makes this a business call, right? I don't do business over the phone. You wanna do business with me, I'll meet you in the park. Fort Greene. By the tennis courts. Thirty minutes. I'll be wearin' a Yankees cap."

"In *Brooklyn?*"

"Ballsy, huh?"

He was, in fact, the only one wearing any kind of a cap. He was short and thin as a rail, another similarity to Aurelio, and his look of cold, bemused contempt had me thinking fondly of my late snitch. He took a moment to assess me, then said coldly, "Okay, whatta you want?"

For a moment I couldn't answer him. There was no trust between us, only the half-hearted recommendation of sorts that Aurelio had given me after I wouldn't pay him enough.

"If you don't wanna talk to me, you're wastin' my time, *gringo,*" he said, and his look of contempt hardened.

"Give me a minute," I said, and he turned his back to look at the empty tennis courts. Then, just as quickly, he turned back.

"Aurelio, he told me some stuff about you, so at least I know you're not a cop. I don't fink for the cops. I don't fink for nobody. I'm a businessman. My business is information. I happen to know, through the grapevine, that you paid to have Aurelio buried proper. So, that's maybe a point in your favor, but that's all."

"It goes both ways," I said.

"What does?"

"Trust."

"I been backstabbed by fuckin' *experts*, man. You understand that?"

"So have I, and a lot more often, I bet."

"Bullshit."

"One of Aurelio's favorite words," I said, smiling for the first time.

"All right, I give you a test run. What you lookin' for?"

So I told him.

"Be here, tomorrow, same time. A hundred. No checks."

"Done," I said. I offered my hand, he looked at it with suspicion for a moment, but then he took it.

20

Rothberg didn't stir from his house during Arnie's watch, so we shifted gears again the next day. He was eager to follow the T-Bird once more that night, and I set my sights on tailing Santini's soon-to-be ex-wife before meeting Enrico Rosario in Fort Greene Park in the afternoon. I was leaving for that very purpose when Maria Santini strolled seductively into my office.

"You remember me?" she asked, taking the client chair on the other side of my desk. She crossed her legs, showing sheer nylon. She was dressed like a movie star at a Hollywood premiere. Bette Davis came to mind.

"Of course," I answered, and sat down. "But that was a long time ago."

"You *do* remember, then?"

"Of course."

"If you're thinking of worrying about it, don't bother," she said, quickly batting her brown eyes. "I don't hold grudges."

"That's good to know."

"I'm the forgive-and-forget type."

"Even better," I said.

"If you remember me, you'd remember Rocco, too."

"Right again. Should I worry about that?"

"Hardly. Rocco, he was just my stud horse of the moment back then. I didn't miss him much when he was gone. There were plenty of other capable guys around, and you ratting us out to my father, that was a swell way for me to escape that stupid convent he wanted to send me to. I mean, do you think I could I *ever* be a nun?"

"I guess a belated 'thank you' is just as good as a timely one," I said. "And no, you could never be mistaken for a nun."

"So, you're forgiven, on both counts."

"But that's not the reason for your visit," I said, watching her face carefully as I said it. Looking for deceit.

"Quite true. I wish to employ you."

"Say again?" I said.

She stopped to admire herself in a pocket mirror for a moment, took another moment to find her lipstick in her leather purse, and reworked her full lips until they were the brightest red. She gave me a look that stopped just short of 'come hither.' It was almost mesmerizing, watching her work.

"Isn't that the word for it?" she asked, in a coy, almost little girl voice. "Employ? Hire?"

"That's the right word," I said. "But for what reason?" I felt myself stiffening somewhat in my chair, pushing back, hoping to hear it make a reassuring squeak. It didn't make a sound.

"I'm being blackmailed. Well, actually, my stepmother is being blackmailed."

"By whom?"

"Correct grammar. Very nice."

"You were saying..."

She laughed. "My psychiatrist, as strange as that might seem. Dr. Meyer Rothberg. You may have heard of him. He has a somewhat elite clientele."

I tried not to react. "What does he have on your stepmother?"

"My parents are getting divorced. My mother has been seeing Dr. Rothberg *socially*, if you understand my meaning."

I did, but I offered a look of confusion anyway. A contest of wills had just begun, and it was safer -- and more to my advantage -- to look dumb at first.

"He's been *fucking* her. Okay? Come to think of it, I suppose he could blackmail me, too, and for the same reason, if he thought about it some. Maybe it'll come to that. At any rate, the settlement my stepmother expects to receive will be, shall we say, compromised, if word leaks out that she'd been unfaithful to my father. The magistrates don't like to hear negative stuff like that in Divorce Court, and the good doctor apparently has a hidden Dictaphone in his office."

"How much is he demanding?"

"A hundred thousand. Not that he needs the money. He has a house on Albemarle Road, for God's sake. Almost as big as my father's. But he's enjoying the power that he has over her. Over both of us, I expect."

"Have you made any payments yet?"

"Two. The first was at some shabby little printing shop over in Brownsville. The second was at a bar in Flatbush. The Crazy Horse, I think it's called. Why he picked those places, I'll never know. But that's where I went when I paid his agent. He never would come himself."

"And the agent was?"

"Don't know him. Never saw him before I went to the print shop. A small, chubby fellow in his forties. Pencil mustache. Creepy, and then some."

Again, I tried not to react. "And at the bar?"

"Same person."

"And how much do you still owe?"

"Half, but he says he doesn't want it now. I think he wants to bleed us dry, slow and steady, the both of us. I've already made two trips to the bank to get his money. My mother's trying to hide some of hers away at a Swiss bank so he can't get it all."

"You haven't been to the police, then?"

"Of course not."

"And what is it you want me to do?"

"Get something on *him*, of course. Something to make him call the whole thing off."

"And that would be?"

"I think he swings both ways in the bedroom. My father's lawyer is queer. *You* know. A homosexual. I think Dr. Rothberg has visited him on occasion, *socially*. Have you ever heard of a fag bar called Julius'? Well, my father's attorney has been known to show up there dressed as Marie Antoinette or Little Orphan Annie, and Dr. Rothberg might be meeting him there. In disguise, of course."

"I see."

"Do you?"

"Well, from what you just told me about you and your stepmother, Dr. Rothberg would seem to be enthusiastically *heterosexual*. You're saying that he has an equally strong appetite for men?"

"That's what I'm saying," she said, eyeballing me.

"All right, let's say that's a given. What's your plan of attack?"

"Simple. Get some compromising photographs of them together, like the kind you took of Rocco and me back at that bar at Coney, and do it before the good doctor decides to gouge my stepmother and me for more money. That might be enough to put an end to it. I'll pay you well, of course."

"Does your father know about this?"

"Of course not. That's the whole point, him *not* knowing about it. Otherwise my poor stepmother will get next to nothing from the divorce settlement. Don't you understand? Look, I'm very fond of my stepmother. I think Father has treated her miserably, and I want her to get what she deserves after putting up with him all these years."

"Has she cheated on him with anyone else?"

"Sure."

"You know this for certain?"

"Of course. We share everything, my stepmom and me, sometimes even the same guys."

"All right," I said, trying to look nonchalant. "I charge fifty dollars a day, plus expenses. If I meet with any success, I'll call you. Is there a special number you'd like me to call? A private line, perhaps?"

"The phone at the house would be fine," she said, "And if you get results, there's a nice, fat bonus in it for you. Say, five grand?" She stood up. As with everything else, she did it with perfect grace. She'd come a long way from the homely teenaged girl who'd taken a ride on Rocco Gabriano's dick outside the Steeplechase Bar at Coney. She was elegant now, movie star beautiful. But cold. Cold as a stone.

"All right, then," I said, and stood up.

136

"There's one more thing," she said after a pause. "One more *important* thing. If the good doctor finds out, one way or another, that I'm -- what's the phrase again? -- ratting on him, he won't hesitate to have me snuffed. He knows people who know people who do that sort of thing."

"I'll try to be as discreet as possible," I said. "And so will any operatives that I put on the case."

She showed me a look of disappointment, followed by a pause, followed by a come-hither look. "You mean, you can't just do it all by yourself?"

"It's always better to have some back-up," I said. "Just in case things get a little complicated."

"Very well. And a good day to you, Mr. Lombardi."

"Good day," I said.

"I'm counting on you, you know," she added, displaying herself for a moment in the doorway.

"Not to worry," I said.

"I *never* worry," she said, and she walked out.

I watched her from the office window as she walked to her car. Watched her put on her white driving gloves. Watched her check her lipstick and makeup in the rear view mirror. Watched her drive away in the pink T-Bird. I was Alice again, for better or worse, looking the wrong way through the looking glass.

Arnie didn't start his shift until the evening, and I was hoping that he wouldn't come to the office early because I didn't want to tell him what I'd just heard from Maria Santini. It certainly explained her recent trips to Brownsville and Flatlands, and her stepmother's visit to the Williamsburg Savings Bank as well. I still couldn't figure out the two trips to the marshes over by Jamaica Bay, but everything else seemed to fit into place. Once again, Santini's story seemed to lose credibility. And Charlie's death was just a deep hole of a mystery that kept getting deeper. I had no idea how to break the news to Arnie if he did stop by, so I left for my meeting with Enrico Rosario.

I arrived at the tennis courts at Fort Greene Park just past the appointed meeting time, hoping I wasn't too late. I waited almost an hour without success, and then I called him from the office.

"Sorry," I said. "I was detained."

"I don't wait for nobody," he said.

"I understand. Can we try again?"

"Tomorrow," he said, gruffly. "Same time."

And he hung up.

I spent the rest of the afternoon waiting for Wanda Santini, the soon-to-be ex-wife, to drive out past the cast-iron gates of Santini's castle, hoping I wasn't wasting my time again. The Barracuda Brothers had given me a clear motive for murder as far as she was concerned, but she'd done nothing to advance that idea further. Viper –– make that 'Aabidullah' –– had already pointed out that her murder of Santini would be at cross-purposes to getting a decent divorce settlement. It was hard to disagree with that idea, as much as I might like to, given the source. Maria Santini had said the same thing. But Mrs. Santini went exactly nowhere, and so, after four hours of doing nothing, I returned to the office.

Arnie came in an hour later, looking depressed. I was still reluctant to tell him about Maria Santini's visit, but I had to. He froze in place when I explained it all to him.

"Jesus," he said. "Jesus Christ."

"I would've told you sooner," I said, "but... "

"Jesus."

"Kind of throws a big monkey wrench into all of our fine-tuned shamus machinery, doesn't it?" I said.

"She just walked in? Just like that?"

"Just like that, partner."

"And you agreed to work for her?"

"We didn't sign any papers, and I didn't take an advance, but yes, I suppose I did."

"Jesus," he said. "And the lawyer and the shrink, they're...?"

"She's of the opinion that the shrink, like the lawyer, is a switch hitter in the great national pastime of sex, but… Anyway, I'm being paid to check it out."

"You mean *we're* being paid," said Arnie, showing some petulance.

"Okay. *We're* being paid."

"Can't we just lean a little on the guy first?"

"Which one?"

"Either."

"No can do. She thinks if the good doctor finds out that she's put somebody on to him, he'll have her killed. Then again, if we lean on the lawyer, and *he* squeals to the shrink, it's the same thing. So, we have to finesse it."

Arnie frowned. "I never did get used to that damn word," he said.

"Well, maybe you'd better."

"And in the meantime?"

"Follow the T-Bird tonight, but don't get too close."

"We're back to square one, aren't we?"

"Not even," I said.

I wasn't quite ready to go home after my talk with Arnie, so I left the office when he did, bid him good night, and took a slow, contemplative walk down New Utrecht Avenue. The streetlights were just coming on, and the night air was crisp and clean as it wafted in off the ocean. One of my old haunts, Bernard's Billiards, had occupied one of the storefronts along this street. It hadn't been a pool hall for years. The *paisano* who'd once owned it, Victor Iademarco, had been a good man and a good friend. The psychotic named Jack Janus had murdered him almost a year ago, murdered him for no other reason than Janus' consuming hatred of me; but Victor wasn't the only reason why I remembered the place so fondly. It was at Bernard's that I'd first met Johnny Temafonte, Laura's younger brother. He was thoroughly shit-faced at the time, losing badly at eight ball, and about to get a well-deserved beating from a pair of Neanderthal thugs when Frankie and I stepped in to rescue him. If it hadn't been for Bernard's, I'd never have met his more sensible sister Laura, who would become my wife and the mother of my children. I wondered as I walked the familiar street what my life would have been like if I'd never met her. More like Arnie's, probably. He had two unhappy marriages behind him, and an incompleteness of heart and mind that comes from not finding the right woman. Marriage can complicate the life of a shamus more than anything else on the planet, and I often had to remind myself that I was a husband and father first -- that being a private detective was a livelihood, not a life. That wasn't always the way things played out in real time in the real world, but that was what I always came back to in contemplative walks like this. So, I wandered the few blocks that it took to set my rudder straight again, and quickened the pace back to my house on 16th Avenue. It was almost the dinner hour for Edward Lombardi and his family, and after that it was going to be story time. Life didn't get any better than that.

21

Arnie came in early the next morning. I hadn't been expecting him at that hour, so I gave him a peevish look.

"And what are *you* doing here?" I asked as he poured himself a cup of lukewarm coffee.

"I didn't follow her last night," he said. "I didn't follow anybody." There was no apology in the tone.

"Oh? You might have told me."

"I figured to go and get drunk someplace, but I couldn't even do that. So sue me. And you?"

"I went home."

"Jesus. We're spinnin' our wheels so hard, pretty soon we'll be drivin' on the goddamn rims."

"I had the strangest feeling, even after I went to bed last night, that there were wheels in motion already on this thing. Wheels in motion, partner. I was just some kind of bystander watching it go by in slow motion and not making any sense of it. I couldn't shake the feeling. It was like I was some minor character in a B movie that the audience wouldn't even miss if he didn't show up."

"That's too fuckin' deep for me," Arnie admitted, and sat down heavily in the chair reserved for my clients. The chair Maria Santini had sat in the day before. I usually chided him about things like that, but there was no point in calling him on his bad habits now.

"So, what do we do," he asked. "While this big wheel is rollin'?"

"Try not to fall under it, I guess."

"Amen to that, brother."

"There are still some loose pieces to the puzzle," I said after I settled in behind my desk. "Still some possibilities."

"You're telling me?"

"One of them is Dial Printing. I'm going to see that guy Rosario this afternoon. It's probably a lot of nothing, but I've already agreed to pay him."

"The new snitch?"

"The one Aurelio sort of recommended."

Arnie stretched his arms and legs to their extremities and yawned.

"Why don't you take the day off," I said.

"I could keep an eye on the shrink if you want."

"Even at Julius'?"

"Sure," he said. "I can handle it."

"Actually, I doubt it," I said, smiling shamelessly at him. "Besides, we'll need Liam for that particular job. He's good with a camera, especially the kind you can hide up your sleeve. Santini's daughter wants some incriminating pictures as proof."

"So, Liam's in?"

"He's in. He's on salary."

Arnie smiled savagely. "You gonna send him to Julius' dressed like a ballerina or something?"

I smiled back. "A sailor, maybe. Or a lumberjack. He could handle that. Then again, you don't really need a costume to go in there. Just ask the Barracuda Brothers."

"Wish I coulda been there for that," he said, grinning. "A fly on the wall."

"You might still get your chance."

A brief silence set in. "Coffee's gone bitter," he said, and put the cup down.

"The Bella Italia's open," I said.

"You really believe her? Santini's daughter, I mean."

"I don't know," I said.

"If her story adds up, then..."

"Still a lot of loose pieces, Arnie."

"Yeah."

"Like a big jigsaw puzzle. Can't put it together if you don't have all the parts."

"Or if somebody mixed the boxes up."

"Amen, partner."

I was still early for my meeting with Enrico Rosario, so I left Arnie at the office and went home for a while. Laura was running the vacuum cleaner in the entry hall. Mary was up in the playroom with her dollhouse, and Amanda was at St. Margaret's, my *alma mater*, preparing herself for Harvard or Yale. I took a seat at the kitchen table. Laura turned off the vacuum cleaner and wandered into the kitchen. The look on her face was both curious and calm.

"To what do I owe this honor?" she asked with a half-smile. She sat across from me.

"A lull in the action," I said.

"Is that what it is?"

"I'm wondering if Gino still has that job opening at the market. I might just take it this time."

"Well..."

"You used to *want* me to take it," I said. "And I know he could use some help with two of his kids in college now. Assistant Store Manager –– that would be my official title."

"You'd be miserable," she said.

"I'm miserable now."

"You'd be worse."

"Maybe I could sell Buster Brown Shoes or real estate. Shelve books at the public library like you used to."

She frowned seriously. "Are you going to just sit here and whine?"

"I have to meet a guy."

"By all means, then, go meet him," she said, and turned on the vacuum cleaner.

I went back to Fort Greene Park, by the tennis courts. There were benches there, and I was already tired, so I sat down. A light spring mist was falling. Not enough to require an umbrella or a raincoat, and refreshing in a way, cleansing. Nobody was on the courts; it wouldn't be tennis weather for at least another month. I was there at the appointed hour this time, but Enrico Rosario failed to show up. I waited a half-hour, and then I decided to call it off.

Maybe Nick DeMassio could recommend a new snitch for me. The cops seemed to know them a lot better than I did. I was standing up to leave when I felt a bony hand on my shoulder. Enrico Rosario was right behind me. His face was without expression.

"Sit down," he said, and sat on the bench with me.

"You're late," I said, giving him a hard look. "One thing I can say for Aurelio, he was never late, and he always had something useful to tell me."

"And where were *you* yesterday?"

"Detained," I said. "I told you."

"That's the same as being late, isn't it, *gringo*? I can take my information and walk," he said. "If that's the way you want it."

"So you have something?"

"Would I be here if I didn't?"

"All right," I said, and he stuck his hand out.

"First, the hundred," he said.

"Without any information, fifty."

"All right."

I waited as he counted the bills and stuffed them deep into his coat pocket.

"The building belongs to a guy named Rothberg," he said.

"I already know that."

"He rents the office space out to Dial Printing," he continued, as if he hadn't been interrupted.

"I know that, too."

"But what you don't know is the guy who rents the space. Now, try to stay with me, okay, *gringo*? His name is George W. Brent. He's got no current aliases, but he's got a long history of using different names." He pulled a piece of folded tablet paper from his coat and read them to me: "Donald Sanderson, Michael Torino, Edward Michaels, Thornton Smith... Can you believe that? -- *Thornton*? Then there's James J. Gilroy, Samuel Hicks, Harry..."

I held up my hand to stop him. "Okay, so the guy's changed his name a bunch of times. So what? Has he got a record?"

"He has. And can you guess what for?"

144

"Am I paying you so I can guess?" I said, scowling.

"He's a forger. If you need a phony driver's license, a new Social Security card, a passport, a military ID, whatever, George W. Brent is your boy."

"And you think Rothberg knows what he's up to?"

"Maybe he didn't at first. Maybe he found out and George had to cut him in. But I'm betting he's in. It's a nice little second income, tax-free, and from what I hear, George's work is first-rate. Does it upstairs, though. Not in the shop. That's where he lives. Upstairs."

"There's a woman who works there," I said.

"Name's Sanders. Nora Sanders. She's clean. Probably has no idea she's working for a master forger."

"Guy with a pencil mustache -- he work there, too?"

"No. Why?"

"Just asking. And the local cops?"

"Either they're taking their own cut, or they don't have a clue. This is Brownsville, remember."

"All right," I said, and stood up.

"Well, is it good enough? What I found out?"

"It's good enough."

"Then, if it's all the same to you, *gringo*, I'll take that other fifty now."

Arnie was still in the office when I got back. He was building a delicately stacked house of cards in the middle of my desk. When I slammed the door, on purpose, the house collapsed.

"You're in a bad mood," he said. "Me, too. Maybe we need a drink. How about Nero's? I'm buying."

"What's today?" I asked.

"May 5th."

"No, I mean what day of the week?"

"Friday. So, you wanna go to Nero's? Or the Tip-Top?"

"You don't have a date?" I asked.

"In the middle of the afternoon? Are you kidding? Got one tonight, though. Real hot number."

145

"Maria Santini, perhaps?"

"Naah. Let up on her, will ya?"

"You've developed an attachment?"

"I wish."

"She's as cold as a tombstone, Arnie. Maybe yours."

"You just can't figure her out, that's all."

"And you can?"

"Changed my mind about her, that's all. I think she's clean."

"That's very generous of you," I said.

We had a couple of beers at Nero's, and I went home early. In the meantime, Arnie and Liam had time off while I figured out a way to snare Dr. Rothberg. It was a one-man job, Liam's mostly, and the work would most likely be done at night inside and outside Julius'. I wasn't entirely sure why I was doing it. I wasn't happy to have Maria Santini for a client, but she would pay well, and there are times in my business when that is the only thing that matters.

I had a quiet dinner with the family that night, read the next chapter of *Anne of Green Gables* to Amanda and Mary, and put them to bed just after eight. That was when the trouble started.

"We're overdrawn on the checking account," Laura said when we were on the couch in front of the television. It was eight-thirty, and *Route 66* was on. Todd and Buzz drove a Chevy Corvette, so I was jealous.

"That's not possible," I said.

"Well, it is. I got the notice from the bank just today."

"I know the balance was low, but... You didn't deposit the money Santini gave me, minus what I set aside to pay the guys?"

She frowned, but it was not an apologetic frown. "*That* money?"

"Yes," I said, flatly. "*That* money."

"Well..."

"That's more than seventeen hundred dollars, Laura. The IRS will want to know where it came from. You recorded it in the books, didn't you?"

The frown deepened. "No."

"And you didn't deposit it?"

"No. It's in your nightstand drawer in the bedroom."

"Why?"

She eyeballed me. "It's dirty money, Eddie."

I eyeballed her back. "I earned it cleanly," I said.

"But your Mr. Santini didn't. It's *his* money. And it has blood all over it. I don't want that kind of money paying for our children's education, or their toys, or their clothes, or even their daily bread."

I stood up, walked to the television, and turned it off. "We don't exactly have money to burn, Laura."

"We do now," she said, coldly.

"You're joking, right?" I said. Her steely look gave me the answer.

"There's even a book of matches in the drawer," she added. "Next to the money. For when you decide that the time's come."

"When *I* decide?"

"It's your money, Eddie, not ours. It's not money that will ever belong to this family."

"Why are you telling me this now?" I said, my voice rising.

Her steely look weakened, but only slightly. "You had other things on your mind."

"I still do," I said, stiffening.

I didn't wait for a response. I walked out of the house and took a long, troubled walk through the neighborhood. I was glad I hadn't told Laura about working for Santini's daughter, although no money had as yet changed hands. For the first time since taking Santini's money, I felt dirty myself. But then I had another thought. When you're a shamus, sometimes you have to check your idealism at the door. I had myself committed crimes of a sort, including murder. I could file those things under "collateral damage," or "occupational hazards," or "situation ethics," but they still left a mark that stung sometimes.

When I got home, well past midnight, Laura was asleep. I took a moment to open the drawer to my nightstand, saw the neat stack of bills and the matchbook, and closed the drawer again. Then I went to bed.

22

The problem hadn't resolved itself the next morning, but Saturday gave us both a chance to think on it separately. Amanda and Mary watched their favorite cartoon shows and *Captain Kangaroo* until almost noon. Then Laura took them to visit the Temafontes, their maternal grandparents, who had agreed to treat them to an afternoon on the kiddie rides at Coney Island. For me, it was just another workday, with one extra burden to carry.

I arrived late enough to find Arnie and Liam waiting in the office. The brazen looks they gave me quickly turned to peals of laughter.

"We just decided, Eddie lad," Liam announced. "On this Rothberg thing. In place of Liam, we're going to send you into Julius', dressed like Mae West."

"*Come up and see me sometime, pretty boy,*" added Arnie in his best falsetto, and the laughter increased by a few decibels.

"Count me out," I said. "And can we talk about the actual plan now?"

Arnie grinned. "You mean there's an actual plan?"

"There is," I said. "So, listen up."

And they did. My part was to drive to Albemarle Road to see if Dr. Rothberg had plans for the evening. Arnie was to watch the lawyer's house in Brooklyn Heights and follow him if he went anywhere. Liam, mini-camera at the ready, would be inside Julius', waiting for us. If both the shrink and the lawyer left for the evening, and if they both ended up at Julius', we were on. If only the lawyer showed, the operation was off. If Dr. Rothberg showed up alone, which I still had trouble imagining, then Liam could take pictures of him. Maria Santini would have the evidence she needed to call off the blackmail game he'd been playing with her and her stepmother. We wouldn't need Fanucci in that case. Meyer Rothberg's presence at Julius' would be more than enough social incrimination. But for the next three days, none of those things happened.

The morning of the fourth day, we met again in my office. Their collective grim mood matched mine. Even Arnie's desire to find his buddy's killer was not enough to keep this thing going much longer. Finally, I got tired of listening to the two of them whine.

"This is the very last night we're doing this," I announced. "I've got another case coming up, a private matter that I won't need either of you for." I didn't tell them that it was the business of Gino's daughter and her beatnik boyfriend, even though I had no plans to pursue that case, either. It was just an easy out for me. "And you two don't need to be hanging around here now. I've got paperwork to do on the Santini business. You'll just distract me. So get yourselves lost for a while, but be ready to track the usual suspects from around seven tonight. You've got the camera, Liam?"

He nodded.

"Okay, then, this is positively the last time we're doing this. Unless the two of them wind up at Julius', or just the good doctor, the operation is over. Finished. *Kaput.*"

As they left, I took my Smith-Corona portable from the top of the filing cabinet and put it on my desk. I sat in my big swivel chair, spun myself around a couple of times, and then stared helplessly at the blank sheets of paper stacked next to the typewriter. Time passed, and I looked up at the clock. It was just after eleven, not quite lunchtime. I ambled downstairs to the Bella Italia Luncheonette, grabbed a newspaper, and propped it against the typewriter. I hadn't written a word of the report, and I wasn't in the mood to start. I was done with the newspaper around noon, so I paid a second visit downstairs, returning with a Coke and a grilled cheese sandwich. I began thinking about Enrico Rosario again, thinking about wheels set in motion. Was Dr. Rothberg aware that the man renting the space in his building –- George W. Brent, or whoever –- was running a bogus ID operation upstairs, and if he did know, had Maria Santini gone to Dial Printing to pay blackmail money to her psychiatrist or to buy herself some phony paperwork? And why would she do that? She'd be paying me a lot of money to get dirt on Rothberg before he presumably got to her, but then Santini had paid me a lot of money also.

To do what?

I'd told Liam and Arnie that the surveillance was over after tonight, but I still wasn't sure myself that it was. The case just wouldn't go away. After staring at the Smith Corona and my unfinished report, I drove out to Jamaica Bay again, back to where Maria Santini had gone in her pink T-Bird, back along the marsh roads. What was I looking for? I didn't know. It was just that feeling again that something was going on in plain sight, but I couldn't see it. So I drove back to the office. Laura and the kids were probably back home from Coney, and it was a full two hours before I was expected to drive to Albemarle Road again, but I didn't move from my office chair. I stared at the untyped report, looked mindlessly out the window at 18th Avenue, and waited until it was time to go to work.

It was dark when I arrived at Rothberg's. Lights were on inside the house, and his car, a late model Cadillac, was parked in the big, circular driveway. I wondered again about Maria Santini's claim that the doctor was a switch hitter in the bedroom. That didn't jibe with what Aurelio Rodriguez had told me about him. A stud horse, he'd said. A ladies' man. Outward appearances could be deceptive, but everything my late snitch had said about him made me think the opposite. If there was any truth to the story, I had the feeling it was somewhere in between their two versions of it. Or somewhere else entirely.

It was past eight and I was ready to leave when he finally came out of the house, got into his car, and drove away. To Julius', maybe? Finally? He drove across the Brooklyn Bridge into Manhattan. That was a promising sign; but instead of stopping in Greenwich Village, he drove into Midtown, pulled up outside the Plaza Hotel on Fifth Avenue, left the car with a valet, and walked into the lobby. When he came out, ten minutes later, a young woman who looked like a movie starlet was on his arm. I didn't even bother to follow them. I just watched them drive away and redirected myself back toward West 10th Street and Julius'. It was time to put a disappointing end to a frustrating case.

23

I saw Arnie's car first. It was parked almost a block away from Julius'. God forbid any of his friends should see him, even on the job, anywhere near a place that catered to homosexual men. Liam, who was just as straight as Arnie but entirely unconcerned about appearances, had parked right across the street from the building. There was only a small crowd outside, but I was sure that the joint was probably jumping on the inside. I opened the passenger door of Arnie's car and sat next to him.

"Well, the lawyer's here," Arnie explained. "But you can forget about the Bo Peep costume. He's wearin' a regular suit."

"The psychiatrist is on a date," I said. "With a woman. He won't be here, and that's a fact."

"Then I guess nothin' much is gonna happen," said Arnie. "You sure the daughter said he swung both ways?"

"Yes," I said, "and the idea's starting to bother me."

Arnie gave me a puzzled look. "You think she made it up?"

"I'd like to think she didn't, but she's Jimmy Santini's daughter, and Deception is probably her middle name. In Italian, of course."

Arnie opened the door and stepped out into the street. "I guess I better get Liam," he said, grinning. "Before he goes over to the other side."

"That'll be the day," I said.

"That's a song," said Arnie.

I frowned back at him. "Just go get Liam," I said.

"Guy who wrote it got killed in a plane crash."

"Just go get Liam."

I watched him walk into Julius', and then I turned my attention back to the few men who were gathered outside. I was thinking about Laura and the kids again and about a certain stubborn shamus named Eddie Lombardi who had a lingering idea in his head that he couldn't shake. I wanted him to give up on that idea, but it kept nagging. So many ways to be duped, and it was always guys like me who seemed most likely to fall for this kind of trickery, for the little twisted schemes that the opposition could cook up with so little effort. I was being tricked, all right. I just couldn't identify the trickster.

It was the sudden commotion from inside Julius' that derailed my train of thought. Men were pouring out and running in all directions. I ran from the car, made for the entrance, but there was no way to get past the surging crowd. In the panic, I was pushed back all the way to the edge of the sidewalk. Finally, I grabbed one of the men and pulled him toward me.

"What's going on?" I shouted, but all he could shout back was, "Cops!" before he wriggled away. I couldn't see Arnie or Liam. They might have taken the fire exit out, I thought, but that was at the back of the building, so I kept trying to move forward. Finally, pushing past the last of the crowd, I made my way in. The place was almost empty now, but there were several bodies on the floor, men who had been trampled in the panic. Two were motionless beside the entrance, and another was curled up and groaning under a table. I looked again for Arnie and Liam, but it wasn't until I was almost at the back exit that I saw them at the end of the bar. Liam was bleeding from a cut just above his right ear, and Arnie was dabbing it with a bar towel.

"You okay?" I asked, looking past Arnie at Liam. He didn't respond, but his eyes were open. I'd been talking into his deaf ear, so I moved. "You okay?" I asked again, and this time he nodded and tried to smile. I turned to Arnie. "Can he get up?" I asked, and Arnie nodded. In a minute, we had Liam outside the building and leaning unsteadily against the back wall.

"We gotta move," said Arnie. "Cops'll be here any minute."

"What happened?"

"Somebody shouted that the vice cops were on the way, and the whole place went nuts. It took me a while to find Liam in the crowd. They were all crazy tryin' to get to the exits. Then I found him, back there beside the bar."

"There aren't any cop cars outside," I said. "Not one. You sure somebody shouted that it was the cops?"

"Yup. Loud and clear. A telephone call to the bar, I'm guessin'. So, they're not comin'?"

"Well if they weren't before, they will be now, with all this commotion," I said. "Let's get some distance, see if we can find a luncheonette or something nearby. If the cops find us here, they'll tie us up for hours with questions."

"Okay," said Arnie, giving Liam a shoulder up.

"Glad you agree, partner," I said, smiling. "Just think what would happen to your love life if you got busted in a homo vice raid."

We found a small deli a couple of blocks over on Bleeker Street. We could hear the sirens now. Our three cars were still on West 10th Street, and it bothered me that the cops might check the registrations. It was clear that the cops were responding to a riot rather than to Julius' as a den of sin. The vice squad didn't announce their arrivals with sirens.

So it had been a hoax, a false alarm. But why? And who had made the phony phone call that started the panic? My shamus brain was working overtime again, and again it was coming up empty.

We waited for almost an hour drinking coffee before returning to our cars. There was yellow police tape across the entrance, and two uniformed cops were standing outside. The men who'd been injured in the panic had probably been carted away to hospitals, and the onlookers had drifted away in search of other amusement. The regulars of Julius' were long gone.

Liam insisted that he was okay to drive, so we all went back to the office. I made coffee despite the fact that we'd drunk gallons of it at the deli. We fixed a bandage for Liam's head, decided that he didn't need stitches, and reviewed the evening's events.

"You believe me now?" said Arnie, suddenly glaring at me.

"About?"

"This whole thing. This Santini business."

"Explain, please," I said.

"*Come on*, Eddie. Somebody *knew* we were gonna be there. *Us*. Somebody knew. That's what the phony phone call was about. Somebody's been fuckin' with us."

"Arnie, every guy -- every *regular* -- in there was a reason for the cops to raid the place. Vice cops, anyway. They couldn't care less why we were there."

"Truth be told," said Liam.

"But, why..."

"Jesus! Wait a minute!" I said, just short of shouting. "Fanucci, the lawyer! Jesus Christ!" I looked hard at Liam. "Was he anywhere near you when the riot started? Could you see him?"

Liam had to think about that. Finally, he said, "Just before, but then he wandered off with some guy toward the other end of the bar. Young, tall guy. I didn't see him afterward."

"And I didn't see him come outside. Not even somebody who remotely *looked* like him. You say that he was walking toward the front of the building when you last saw him?"

"That he was. The front door would've been his way out."

"And I didn't see him."

"*Jesus!*" said Arnie. "If he didn't get out, then..."

"He got stomped in the panic," said Liam.

"I'm betting more than that," I said. "Much more. I'm betting somebody didn't *want* him to get out of that place. Not in one piece, anyway. Somebody who maybe had a score to settle."

"Fanucci -- *he* was the reason for the riot?"

"And the phone call that started it."

"So, what do we do?" asked Arnie.

"*We* don't do anything. *I* pick up this phone," I said, pointing to it, "and I call every hospital in the area. I'm a concerned relative, see? I heard about the riot and want to know if my loved one, Cousin Giorgio, was among those admitted."

"Will they do that?"

"A nurse might. Anyway, it's worth a try."

Lenox Hospital was first on the list. It was the closest, and we didn't have to look further.

"Yes," said the duty nurse. "A Mr. Fanucci was admitted this evening. However..."

"Yes?"

"He was, unfortunately, dead on arrival."

"Trampled?" I asked.

"I'm sorry," she said. "I can't answer that question. It's a police matter."

24

The headline in the morning paper made it official: MURDER AT GAY BAR. I was still reading the story when Arnie appeared in the office doorway. Liam was at home in Midwood, recovering. I didn't expect him to come to work any time soon.

"So, you know?" asked Arnie.

"Now," I said.

"Not trampled. Stabbed."

"I know," I said.

"A room crowded with people. People who'd rabbit at the first hint of a vice raid. Start a panic, kill Fanucci unnoticed, and slip out with everybody else."

"Pretty slick," I said.

"Told you it wasn't over."

"And now I know that, too, partner."

"And whoever did it waited until we were there. Wanted us as witnesses to it. Or, if you wanna put it another way, fucked with us."

"You're thinking Santini again?"

"Or the Barracuda Brothers."

"Well, it wasn't Rothberg, and that's a fact."

"Maria Santini, didn't she say that Rothberg knew people who knew people who..."

"Yes, she did."

"So, she was telling the truth."

"Maybe."

"One less witness to tell anybody about anything. And that means she could be next on the list."

"But whose list?"

"Santini's, of course."

I felt myself turning in my swivel chair, shaking my head. "I know we're running out of suspects, but..."

"Or the Barracuda Brothers, on their Pop's orders."

"I don't think so."

"We're back to the shrink, then. Maybe he found out that Fanucci was planning to blow his cover as a straight lover and ladies' man. Or maybe it was somebody else, somebody even Santini didn't suspect."

"As long as you're beating the bushes looking for new suspects, Arnie, why not the Easter Bunny or Santa Claus?"

He grinned at me. "Why not?"

"Get yourself a cup of coffee or something. I still have to write the report on this case. Care to help?" We looked at the typewriter at the same time.

"Got some errands to run," said Arnie, grinning. "See you back here in a couple of hours. Okay? Then we can start tailing the Easter Bunny."

"Sure," I said, and he left.

I finished the report in less than an hour, filed it, and placed the Smith-Corona carefully atop the filing cabinet. The report made everything sound final enough, but the case wasn't over. If anything, it seemed to be restarting under its own power. Arnie's deck of cards was still on my desk. I was thinking of building my own house of cards and then knocking it over in frustration. But then the phone rang. It was Nick DeMassio.

"Eddie," he said, minus the usual salutation.

My first thought was that he was calling about Fanucci's murder at Julius', but then I remembered: I'd never actually mentioned Fanucci's name when we'd had our little talk in his office. There shouldn't have been a reason for the call.

"Truth be told, Nick," I answered, thinking of Liam and his host of endearing expressions.

"There's somethin' I think you need to check out in Canarsie," he said, almost casually.

"*Now?*" I said.

"Yeah. Right now."

"Nick, for crying out loud..."

"And it's still *Captain* DeMassio, if you're gettin' ideas. Take the Shore Parkway out until you see a black-and-white parked on the shoulder. Pull in behind it, and then follow the uniformed officer in."

"In *where?*"

"Just follow him. And then get back to me." Before I could add to my protest, he hung up.

I left a note for Arnie when I left, but there wasn't much to say except that I was going to some undisclosed location off Shore Parkway. I wasn't used to taking my marching orders from Nick DeMassio, but then all my rules of shamus engagement had taken a turn lately. Anyway, I had nothing else on the calendar. So I gassed up at the Texaco station and started on the drive eastward.

The black-and-white was waiting for me near Bergen Beach. I pulled in behind it and stopped. A uniformed cop opened the door and walked back to me. He was from a precinct other than Bath Avenue, so I didn't know him. I rolled down the window on the Chrysler.

"You Lombardi?" he asked, and I nodded.

"Okay. Follow me."

It was a narrow dirt road used by sport fisherman to get to the shore of Jamaica Bay. We drove at a slow pace at first until the road widened and some of the deeper ruts smoothed out. It had rained the night before, and there were small puddles in the ruts. There was a parking area at the end of the road, paved with asphalt. There were police cars parked along the side of the road, and a lone vehicle parked at the end of the paved area.

It was a pink T-Bird. There was no driver in it.

"You Lombardi?" asked one of the two detective-lieutenants who stood next to it.

"That's me."

"You know who this car belongs to?"

I shrugged.

"The registration on the sun visor says it belongs to Maria Santini, the mob guy's daughter. You want to tell us why it's here?"

"No idea," I said.

"Captain DeMassio at Bath Avenue thinks you might know."

I shrugged again. "He's entitled to his opinion," I said.

"We think it's a crime scene," said the lieutenant. "Want to come over here for a minute?"

He walked to the T-Bird and waited for me to follow.

"Car's been here since this morning. Late morning, we figure, since the last of the fly fisherman who come here found the car. There's mud on the tires. It rained earlier. Look here at the driver's seat."

I looked. It was damp, and there was blood on it.

"We figure that the lady was pulled from the car by person or persons unknown and transported elsewhere. Maybe dumped in Jamaica Bay. I don't want to use the manpower required to troll for her unless I've got more information. There are no signs she was dragged, and there aren't any signs of a struggle, but..."

"But you think she was taken."

"Forcibly," said the detective. "This part of the parking area is paved, so you can't tell anything from that. But the dirt path the fishermen use to get to the shore is well traveled. She could have been carried along there wrapped in a blanket and left no signs. We found no blood there, anyway, just in the car."

I was still looking at the driver's seat. "There isn't much blood," I said. "Have you noticed?"

"Yeah. We noticed," he said, scowling. "We dusted the car for prints, too. There aren't any. Except on the steering wheel."

"And nowhere else?"

"Nowhere else."

"Don't you find that odd?" I asked. "No prints except on the steering wheel? Even if she took it to a car wash, there'd be prints."

"Beats me, but that's how we found it."

"So, you think her body was dumped in the bay?"

"We won't know unless we start trolling. Or getting some divers out here."

I looked at the abandoned T-Bird again. An idea was forming in my head. "You *really* think she's in the bay?" I said again.

"Where the hell else?" said the detective with some impatience. "Sure, the body might have been taken someplace else, but why bother if the bay's right here. Just weigh her down and dump her and be done with it."

"That would be the easiest way," I said.

"That, or she was driven somewhere else in another car. There were a bunch of cars parked over there in the dirt. Most of them belonged to the anglers, but one of them might have had another purpose. Anyway, it looks like foul play. Kidnapping at the very least, but more likely murder."

"She *was* afraid for her life," I said. "Threats had been made against her. That's what she told me, anyway."

"You'd better explain that," he said, so I did.

"So we should maybe talk to this guy Rothberg?"

"I wouldn't bother," I said.

"You wouldn't bother?"

"Anything he might have had to do with this business is strictly incidental," I said. I knew why now, of course, but as certain as I was, I didn't want any of what I might say showing up on an official police report. Not at the moment.

"Well, why don't you *try* explaining it to us, Lombardi. Captain DeMassio didn't send you here for nothing."

Two uniformed officers appeared along the path that led to Jamaica Bay. One of them looked at the lieutenant, waited for his attention, and then said, "If she was dumped, it wasn't in the shallows. We've been the whole length of the beach. We gonna troll?"

"No," said the lieutenant. "Can you make any plaster casts from those tire marks in the dirt?"

"They criss-cross all over the place," said the cop. "No way to get a clear print of any of the tires."

"I guess we'd better get some divers out here, then," said the lieutenant.

I took another look at the driver's seat and wandered over to the other parking area. I walked a few paces down the dirt path that led to the shoreline. There were plenty of footprints, but no sign of anybody being dragged away. I walked back to the car.

"Well?" said the lieutenant, scowling.

"*If* somebody dragged her away, *if* somebody took her against her will, I can't see any signs of it along the path."

"There wouldn't be any if she was unconscious. Or already dead."

"There's not enough blood for that."

"You said that before."

"And no signs of violence."

"So? You think she just drove her fancy car out here, bled a little, then went for a swim fully dressed, got a cramp, and drowned?"

"No."

"And anyway, what was she doin' way out here in the middle of nowhere?"

"No idea," I said.

"She came here to meet somebody, that's what, and that person killed her."

"Your guess is as good as mine," I said.

"It's *better*, actually. And this *is* a crime scene, until further notice."

"Fine with me. Have you told Santini about this yet?" I asked.

"We had the precinct station call his house. His wife answered, said he wasn't home."

"And how did *she* react?"

The cop scratched his head. "Well, she kinda *didn't*," he said, and gave me a look. "Weird, huh?"

Not the way I was looking at it now. "Well," I said. "I don't think I can help you fellows much more. Don't know why Captain DeMassio thought I could be of any assistance."

"I'll have a long talk with him about that."

"Can I ask a big favor?" I said. "Can you call Bath Avenue and have somebody phone my office for me? We're miles from a pay phone, and I was in the middle of something else with my partner when Captain DeMassio sent me out here. Do you mind? I'd appreciate it."

"If it'll get you out of my hair, Lombardi, I'll be more than happy to do it."

"My partner's name is Arnold Pulaski. He's probably back at my office waiting for me. If he is, can you have Bath Avenue call and tell him to meet me out at the Jones Beach Hotel in Wantaugh? On the double."

"Anything we should know about?"

"No. Just a surveillance case we've been working on. Nothing special."

"All right," said the lieutenant with a deepening frown. I smiled back limply. I'd just added another cop to the unending list of those who didn't like me, but I was okay with that. Because I had all the information I needed now. I drove away on the dirt road at a casual pace until I was back at the Shore Parkway, and then I drove like a demon toward Wantaugh.

To keep an unscheduled appointment with an assassin.

25

It was getting dark when I pulled up outside the Jones Beach Hotel. It was a clear night, the temperature was mild, and the winds were calm. Once again, there were only two cars in the parking lot. Jimmy Santini knew my car by now, so I parked at the curb half a block down from the hotel. There I waited, impatiently, for Arnie to arrive. I needed him there pronto. I wasn't sure when the evening's activities would start, or what the outcome would be, but I was finally ready for it. I finally had the answers.

Or thought I did.

Arnie arrived an hour later. He pulled up behind me, parked, walked to the passenger side of my car, and settled in.

"Sorry," he said.

"For what?"

"I'm a little late, I guess."

"No, actually, you're still early. At least, I hope so."

"And what are we waiting for?"

"A ghost," I said. "Or maybe a couple of ghosts."

"You wanna explain that?" he said.

"Soon enough, partner. You see those two cars in the parking lot? One of them belongs to Jimmy Santini, and the other belongs to one of his many sex toys."

"We gonna play Peeping Tom?" asked Arnie with a ready smirk.

I smirked back before I answered. "Even more interesting than that. Unless I'm mistaken, somebody's going to try to assassinate Santini in there tonight."

"Oh?"

"But we're going to stop that somebody."

"The sex toy?"

"Only if his heart gives out while he's playing with her." But then I added, "No. It'll be murder, Arnie. Like I said."

"A ghost, huh?"

"It's not as bizarre as it sounds," I said.

"So, Santini wasn't makin' it all up?"

"He wasn't."

"Well, I'll be damned."

"Just be careful. And stay with the plan."

"So, there is one?"

"I was almost half-way through figuring it out when you showed up," I said, and grinned at him.

The desk clerk gave us a nervous look as we entered. As I walked up to him, Arnie took the steps to the third floor. He had his orders.

"Yes?" said the clerk, a skinny kid in his mid-twenties. His bicycle was parked in the corner by the entrance. "May I help you?"

"You may, indeed," I said. I pulled my .38 from the holster under my right arm and let him have a good look at it. He staggered back a step from the counter and froze there. There was an office door just behind him.

"Jesus! I got no money, mister," he said, his lower lip trembling.

"I want the key to the room next to Mr. Santini's," I said in a voice meant to calm him. "That's all."

"Mr. Santini?"

"He's the one. He the only one here tonight?"

"Uh, yes," he said, his lower lip firming up.

"Sure about that?"

He shook his head, and then said after a pause, "Well, I'm not at liberty to say, sir. Mr. Santini wouldn't like it if I...'"

"That's all right, sonny. I already know who's with him. He kind of owns the place, doesn't he?" I said, and the lip quivered again. I pulled my .38 away, and he breathed a little better as he handed me a key. "Fine. That's fine. Now, I want you to go back in there," I said, pointing at the office door. "And I want you to close the door behind you. Keep it closed, and don't come out for any reason except for the one I'm going to give you. Do you understand?"

He nodded.

"Is there a phone back there?"

He nodded.

"Good. If you hear gunshots any time tonight, I want you to call the police. But not until. Do you understand?"

He nodded.

"If someone rings the desk bell out here, I want you to ignore it. Do you understand that, too?"

He nodded.

"Do not leave that room under any circumstances until my friend who just went upstairs comes down and tells you to. His name is Mr. Pulaski. Have you got that?"

He nodded.

"Can you lock that door?"

He nodded.

"Good. Lock yourself in," I said, and waited until he complied. Then I took the steps up to the third floor, where Arnie was waiting in silence. He was standing at the door to the room next to Santini's, the room the Barracuda Brothers had used so many times to monitor their father's sexual activities. I handed him the room key, he opened the door, and stepped quietly inside. It was my move next. I walked softly to the door of Santini's room and stood in front of it for a moment, listening. Then I rapped hard.

"Get lost, sonny," Santini shouted from inside. "Can't you tell I'm busy here?"

"This is Eddie Lombardi," I said in a calmer but still determined voice. "Open the door, Jimmy."

For a moment, there was only silence. Then the woman he was with squealed excitedly, and I heard someone getting hurriedly out of the bed. In another moment, the door opened a crack. Santini, dressed in a monogrammed white bathrobe, was glaring at me.

"Good evening, Jimmy," I said.

"You got a death wish or somethin', Lombardi?" he said, tightening the cloth belt on the robe. "What the hell are you doin' here?"

"It's tonight," I said.

"*What's* tonight?" he asked. He turned to the woman. "And quit *bawlin'*. I *know* this guy." Then he turned back to me and said, "Wish to hell I didn't."

"Listen up, now, Jimmy. I want you and the...young lady...to move to the next room. My partner is in there. He'll protect you."

"From *what*?"

"Your killers. One or both of them. They're coming here, tonight. Any minute now, maybe."

"So, I was right?"

"You were right."

Santini turned again to the woman. "Put some clothes on," he said. "Get decent. We're movin' in next door." He waited for something else from me, but I stood in silence as we both listened to the woman getting out from under the bed sheets and hurriedly dressing.

"So, who'd she hire?" he asked finally. "My fuckin' shrew of a wife. Who'd she hire?"

"Next door," I said, firmly. "Do it now. And my partner is expecting *two* knocks. Just two. Any more, any fewer, and he'll be the one shooting at *you*. Right through the door. You got that?"

"Almost forgot," Santini said, grinning. "You got a temper." Then he turned to the woman. "You decent? Let's go."

"Give me the key to your room first," I said.

He waited for her to come to the door, then pulled it all the way open. She was auburn-haired, slightly on the buxom side, mid-twenties, and scared to death. He let her walk ahead a few steps, glared a moment at me, and then he followed.

"Make no sound in there," I said. "Not a word. No matter what you hear going on next door. And don't come out until I knock or my partner hears my voice. Do what I'm telling you, and you'll both live through this."

"Knew it was the fuckin' wife," he said. "Knew it all along. Her and that goddamn shrink."

I smiled at him, cruelly. "I think you're in for a big surprise on that one, Jimmy. Actually, a pair of surprises."

"Oh?" he said.

"Just get in the room."

I watched him knock twice on the door, saw it open, and he and the woman slipped inside with Arnie.

It was time now to set the trap.

I took a long moment to survey Santini's room. There were extra pillows on the floor next to the bed. I placed them end-to-end on it, then pulled the top sheet over them. Two bodies sound asleep, or so it would appear to Santini's assassins. The room lights were still out, so I turned the table lamp on for a moment to check the chambers in my .38 before turning the light off again and slipping into the darkness. I locked the door and took a position just to the left of the bed, near an end table. All six chambers were full.

I waited.

What do you do when you're expecting a murderer? How do you spend the time? Thinking? Not thinking? For me, it wasn't so different from waiting for combat back in Europe, back in the war. You sat or stood or crouched in silence and tried not to let your fears of the moment overwhelm you. You waited to attack your enemy, or for your enemy to attack you. You worked to slow your breathing, to take deeper, longer breaths when you did breathe. You kept alert, and tense, and yet calm at the same time. No time for woolgathering, for inattention. Alert to every sound, no matter how insignificant. Alert to changes in the atmosphere, and always with a light finger on the trigger. No time to correct your errors when the moment arrived. No time for second thoughts, for recalculating the plan. One chance, that's all you'd get, which was the same chance that your enemy had.

So I waited, and kept my mind alert.

I wondered. Would they both show up? Both ghosts? Would I hear two sets of deliberate footfalls on the stairs and in the corridor, or just one? It was possible that both would show, but they'd planned this so well that one assassin was all they'd need. I had an idea where I'd find the other one tonight after it was over, assuming I had actually figured things out correctly. But that would be the easier part. That was always the easier part. This was the part that worried me. This was the part where something could go terribly, fatally wrong if they had a better plan than I did. Or if they knew of the trap they were walking into, and had already made the necessary corrections. I wasn't even sure they'd know which door to kick open. Maybe the one Arnie was in with Santini and the girl. We hadn't discussed the possibility, and it was too late to talk about it now.

Never underestimate your enemies, Lombardi, I thought. *And especially not the ghostly kid.*

26

I tried to keep track of the time as I waited. It was pitch-dark in the room, and for a moment, in the darkness, I lost track of where I was. I'd left the hall light on before assuming my position, but now I wished I hadn't. When the assassin kicked in the door, the less light the better. And then the doubts swept over me. I wondered if I really had figured it all out correctly, if I'd made my conclusions based on faulty assumptions. What if neither of them showed? Santini would be beyond furious with me if it all came to nothing. Still, I was sure, *had* to be sure. The way I'd figured it, it all had to add up to this. There couldn't be any other explanation.

Yes, there were two ghosts, but only one would show up here tonight. The other would be waiting until the deadly work was done, and then they would fly away -- quite literally -- with new identities and plenty of money in a Swiss bank or two. Their revenge complete, they would live happily ever after somewhere, beyond the law, beyond retribution.

After a while I stopped worrying about time and concentrated instead on timing. Soon the assassin would be standing at the door. He -- or she -- would come quietly, on little cat feet, to kick it in. When it flew open, a fusillade of bullets would rip into the pile of pillows meant to look like the bodies of Santini and his bedmate. With the room in total darkness, and never having seen the place, Santini's assassin would have to guess where the bed was. Silhouetted by the hall light, the shooter would be shooting blind, but I wouldn't. The only question was: how many bullets? Would the gun be a .38 or a .45? I'd be counting to six or eight, depending on the gun. When all the bullets were fired, it would be easy enough to drill whoever was standing in the light of the doorway, but I wanted to take the shooter alive; alive enough anyway to sing like a canary at the precinct station. Of course, it hadn't come to that yet, and I was still worried that I might be discovered in my hiding place near the bed; or that I might be hit by a stray bullet fired wildly into the darkness. There are times when all your training, all your shamus experience and expertise cannot help you, when your gut has to give you the answer. And this was going to be one of those times.

I worried about Santini and the woman in the room next door. He would be calm enough, but what would she do when she heard the approaching footsteps on the staircase? Could Arnie muzzle her in time to keep her from giving the ambush away, or would the gunman hear her cry and know that it was a trap? Would that door be kicked in and not mine?

I heard the footsteps then, very light, in the hallway. A single pair of feet. As light as those steps were, I'd decided that the assassin had to be a man. It would take a strong kick to force the locked door open, and I didn't figure a woman doing that. Next to the nightstand, without much cover, I worried again about a spray of shots rather than a nice neat pattern striking the empty bed. There was no time to seek better cover, so I stayed motionless. When I was sure the shooter was standing right in front of the door, I let my finger rest on the trigger and waited for the door to burst open. I started counting slowly in my head, a little relaxing trick I'd learned back in the Airborne.

One, two, three, four, five...

The door slammed open with a sound almost like a gunshot, but then the real bullets came. I started counting again: one, two, three, four, five, six, seven, and all the bullets centered on the bed. So it was a .45. A pause now. One bullet still unfired. Why was he holding back? Had he seen me in the muzzle flash? I raised my gun, but then he fired the last shot into the empty bed, and I was on him. As we tumbled back into the hallway, I shouted to Arnie in the next room, and he came running. Santini was a step behind. The bimbo was running for the stairs.

I looked at the young man I had pinned to the floor. Arnie had his gun drawn, but he could see that he didn't need it and tucked it back into his shoulder holster. The young man was scowling at me, and then even more fiercely at Santini.

"Know this guy?" I asked Santini as I pulled the man off the floor. I dragged him into the bedroom, sat him in the same chair I'd occupied on my first visit, and turned on the table lamp. Santini followed, a look of complete puzzlement on his face. I looked over at Arnie. "Tell the desk clerk he can come out now," I said. "And if he hasn't called the cops, you'd better do it."

"The girl," Arnie said. "I got her license number. You want me to...?"

"Let her go," I said. "She's got nothin' to do with this. Just make the call."

As Arnie took to the stairs, I looked at Santini again. He was staring at the surly young man in the chair. "Well?" I said.

"That's my chauffeur," Santini said. "But that's impossible. He's dead. He burned up in that fire."

"Remarkable recovery, don't you think?" I said. "Ghost Number One, Jimmy. Whoever died in that fire on Bay Parkway, it wasn't this guy. Makes good sense, though, what he did, when you think about it. He took himself right off your suspect list, and mine. Whoever took his place inside that building -- a pickup in a fag bar somewhere, a bum off the street -- our young friend here made sure there wouldn't be enough forensic evidence to say it wasn't him. Trouble is, the man I had following him recognized him at a bar in Flatbush and tried to call it in. He saw a dead man walking, and that was bad luck for both of them. So, my partner's search for his buddy's killer is over now, and the job you hired me for is almost over." I looked at Santini again. "You really *don't* know who this guy is, do you?"

"Like I said, my chauffeur. But..."

I glanced at the man in the chair. "You want to tell him, Harry, or should I?"

"Go to hell," he said, scowling, without looking up.

"In due time," I said, smiling, and turned my attention back to Santini. "He's a Gabriano, Jimmy. That name ring a bell? He's the cousin of somebody you had whacked back in '47. Rocco Gabriano. One of my operatives took pictures of him screwing your daughter back then, and not long after that, he was a floater in Gravesend Bay with his dick stuffed halfway down his throat. So much for sweet little Maria's chances to be a nun. And that brings us to Ghost Number Two. Your darling daughter. I can tell you where she is right now: at Idlewild waiting for lover boy here to show up so they can skip the country with a lot of your money. New names and phony passports for the two of them, obtained from a print shop in Brownsville. That's right, Jimmy. Your daughter wanted you dead. She was in it from the start, just as soon as this one here told her who he was and what he had in mind for you. I'm betting he wanted to do it sooner rather than later, but your Maria had a better idea, one that would take time and planning, and, with the help of your eager wife, some serious transferring of money. That took a while. But then they were ready. Harry here was already dead, so to speak, so all Maria had to do was set it up like she'd been knocked off, too. I just came from where the cops say it happened, but it didn't."

"No," he said, in as close to a little boy's voice as I'd ever heard him. "No, she wouldn't. Not Maria. She *wouldn't.*"

"The proof is at the airport, Jimmy. At Idlewild. The cops believe she's dead, of course, with her car conveniently abandoned near Jamaica Bay and blood on the T-Bird's upholstery. She fooled them, to be sure, but not me. While the cops would be looking for a body they'd never find, Sandra Dee, or Eleanor Roosevelt, or whatever moniker she's wearing these days, would be on her merry way to someplace very comfortable and very untouchable. Europe, I'd guess. Won't happen now, of course, although I should get myself out there. When her boyfriend here doesn't show by flight time, she'll probably go solo. The money's already waiting for her, and she can always find a new stud horse."

"Jesus Christ," said Santini, looking at me with both puzzlement and newfound respect. "Jesus H. Christ."

"I'm sure He didn't know, either," I said, and left him with his mouth open.

27

She was sitting in the waiting area for a Pan American flight to Paris when she saw me approach. She did not get up. The only movement she made was to cross and uncross her legs. She smiled when she saw me. I wondered for a moment if she might be packing heat, but then I dismissed the idea. As far as Maria Santini was concerned, the plan had already worked. I was just an afterthought, or a mirage, something that was of no real concern.

"Ah, Mr. Lombardi," she said, smiling demurely. "What an unexpected surprise."

"And who am *I* addressing?" I asked.

"Excuse me?" she said.

"Well," I said, taking the seat next to her. "Maria Santini is supposed to be at the bottom of Jamaica Bay, so I was just wondering who *you* were at the moment."

"I'm sure I don't understand," she said, deadpan. I was impressed by the cold casualness of it.

"A look at your passport should answer the question nicely," I said. "Do you mind if I look? Or, I could just go to the passenger list and try to guess which name you've chosen. That might be fun."

"It's a 707. There's quite a passenger list," she said, and there was some come-hitherness in the look.

"Don't want to say?"

She smiled, a little warmer. "Not really."

"Let me guess, then. Your stepmother's name is Wanda. Isn't that right?"

"Yes."

"Ah, but you don't look at all like a Wanda," I said, enjoying the game. "I'll go for Betsy. Betsy Ross. Nice and patriotic."

"Funny," she said, and looked bored for the first time.

"He's not coming, you know," I said. "Harry Appolino. And your father's still alive. Not a scratch on him. I know you must be disappointed, but..."

"I really don't know what you're talking about," she said, but when she fidgeted in the purse to find her cigarettes and light one, I knew I'd cracked her armor.

"He's not dead, of course. Your boyfriend, the chauffeur. He'll stand trial right along with you. And your stepmother as well. She's what's known in the criminal statutes as an accomplice, if you don't know how the law works in situations like this. We'll get the psychiatrist, too, but maybe only for blackmail, and only if he really *was* blackmailing you, which I doubt. It's going to be tough separating all the swell stories you've dreamed up from the truth. Still, this'll make a pretty good haul for the District Attorney's office, all things considered."

"Not if you go along," she said suddenly, and with just as sudden a smile of triumph.

"Go along?"

"With me, of course. To Paris. How would you like to be a certain Charles J. Tomlinson?" she asked.

"Your boyfriend's new name?"

"I have his passport right here."

"Without my picture on it," I said. "But a nice try."

"My own new name is Mary Smith, if you'd care to know. I even have the birth certificate. She's two years younger than Maria Santini. Kind of nice to be *legally* younger."

"Must be," I said.

"And she's not even Italian."

"Too bad," I said. "Italians are the best. Some of them, anyway."

"Ten grand if you just walk away," she said.

"Only ten? You must have ten times that much in your new Swiss account."

"The offer stands," she said. "You won't get another."

"It's a tempting one," I said, "but I really wouldn't know what to spend the money on. I'm not what's known as a big spender. You won't be able to spend it, either, once you're convicted. Then again, maybe your father will reconsider and put you back on his inheritance list. Doing time in women's prison won't be much of a party, won't be like dining at Sardi's or wearing the latest Paris ensemble; but at least when you get out, you won't have to work the counter at Woolworth's, assuming your father forgives you. Me, I'd send you up for life and have you come out as a dried-up old woman on your tenth try at parole."

She looked away for a moment. On the periphery were two uniformed policemen, biding their time.

"If you're curious, I'm the one who called them," I said.

"Not very sporting of you."

"I won't need them if you don't give me any trouble," I said, which brought a sneer to her lips.

"You will have to excuse me, then, if I decide not to go quietly," she answered, eyeing the cops for a moment before glaring back at me.

"Make a ruckus if you like," I said. "It'll make no difference to me, or to them."

"You've thought of everything, haven't you?"

"I do try," I said.

"That day I saw you at your office," she said, rising suddenly. "Did you buy any of it?"

"Your story?"

"Yes."

"Well, it *was* pretty convincing, actually. Even my partner Arnie bought it. The only part I couldn't figure was why you drove out by Jamaica Bay those first two times. But then, when you took the T-bird there this time, and the cops called me, I kind of figured it out. Where'd you get the blood?"

"Nose bleed," she said, and smiled again. "Or was it a paper cut? I don't recall."

"You shouldn't keep your nose so high in the air," I said. "And you should've left more blood. Murder is messier than that. You made another mistake, too. You left fingerprints on the steering wheel, but you always wear white gloves when you drive that car, so there shouldn't have been any prints. Not unless you *wanted* the cops to suspect foul play. Not unless you wanted them to be sure that you were the missing driver. Your prints are on file, I'm assuming."

"At the precinct station. Daddy has always been very protective of me."

"Still, wiping out all the other prints, that was overkill. And amateurish."

"I'll do better next time," she said.

"There won't be one," I said. "The charges will be, among others, felony murder, and conspiracy to commit felony murder. You'll get at least twenty years, unless the jury falls for you or Daddy buys them off, which I doubt."

"We'll see," she said with an assurance that gave me pause for a moment.

"Can't use Mr. Fanucci as your lawyer now, can you, now that he's dead? Then again, I understand he only handled divorce cases."

"He wasn't the only lawyer I know," she said.

"And I bet you've been in bed with all of them, except Fanucci. By the way, who did it for you? Who iced him? Was it Harry? After you phoned in that bogus call about a vice raid at Julius'?"

"Why don't you ask him?"

"Oh, it was Harry, all right. After the guy whose skull he crushed in that building and my partner's buddy Charlie outside the bar, a third murder wouldn't weigh so heavily on his conscience. Why'd you have to get rid of Fanucci?"

"And you don't know?" she said, smirking.

"I can guess. To muddy the waters a bit more, and give some credence to the idea that Meyer Rothberg knew people who knew people who... But that's a damned poor reason to kill somebody."

"Any reason is reason enough sometimes," she said. "Just ask my father."

"Amen to that," I said. I signaled the two cops, and they approached. She saw them coming, but her bland expression didn't change. "You can make that big scene now," I said finally. "Be my guest."

"Any point to it?" she asked, grinning.

"Probably not, unless you're hoping for an insanity defense. I'm told those things work sometimes, especially with pretty young women like you who've got the right lawyer and some acting ability."

"I'll keep that in mind," she said.

"I'm sure you will."

"We could have had some real fun together, you and I," she said, and there was some genuine sadness in the tone.

"Black widow mates don't last long," I said, and I walked away from her.

28

Laura was asleep when I got home. I didn't want to wake her -- and have to explain -- so I sacked out on the living room sofa. I dreamed the sleep of the dead, and the blessed. The sound of the washing machine woke me in the morning. Laura was in the kitchen drinking coffee when I staggered in and took a seat across from her.

"When did you get home?" she asked.

"Late. Just finishing the last few details on the Santini case."

"Gino called," she said over the sound of the washing machine. "He wants you to call him back."

"Oh, no," I said, rubbing the sleep from my eyes.

"Is something wrong?"

I remembered my promise to talk to Gino's daughter about hanging out with beatniks. I was hoping that he'd forgotten, and I dreaded the possibility that he hadn't. "Well..."

"You'd better call him. You know how he gets when you don't."

I decided to confront him in person instead. I walked to the supermarket with his name in blue neon over the door. It was a nicer walk than the one that first day the Santini business started, and although the weather was not in any way ominous, my expectations were. His wife Gina was at the checkout. She smiled at me in a way that told me she was somehow out of the loop about beatniks, or at least the part of the loop that I was in.

"He's down in the stock room," she said without my asking. I smiled back and took the basement stairs. I found him rummaging around the canned goods.

"So, there you are," he said gruffly.

"As instructed," I said, offering a mock salute.

"You didn't talk to Gloria. You didn't talk to my little girl."

"I already told you, Gino. I didn't have the time. Now I do. Do you still want me to talk to her? Or tail her?"

"Too late for that now," he said, fumbling with the cans.

180

"Oh? Did she marry the guy?"

"No. She dumped him. Or he dumped her. I don't really know. Anyway, it doesn't matter."

"Oh? And why is that?"

"Now it's a P.R."

"A *what?*"

"Puerto Rican. She met him at some club in Greenwich Village. A musician, for God's sake. And a goddamn spic."

"Don't let the spic hear you say that," I said, frowning at him. "He might just kick your Eye-talian ass."

"Jesus! Why can't she find a nice Italian boy? There are plenty right here in the neighborhood. My little girl goin' with some greasy spic musician? Come on!"

"The white boys use plenty of grease, too," I said. "Maybe even more than the Puerto Ricans. Even the white boys on *American Bandstand.*"

"Yeah, well..."

I smiled at him, a wry, almost contemptuous smile. "Your little girl, as you call her, appears to be a bit more open-minded than you are," I said. "You might learn a few lessons from her, if and when you ever get your fat head out of your fat Eye-talian ass."

"I don't understand her anymore, Eddie. Swear to God. She's hard and cold. And angry."

"About exactly what?"

"Damned if I know."

"You could work on that if you wanted to," I said.

"I just don't understand her. I used to. But whatever's goin' on with her, I think she's makin' a mistake. A big mistake."

"Let it be hers, then," I said. "And when she finally wises up, you'd better be there for her." Then I walked back upstairs.

A week passed. Business was slow. I gave Arnie some time off, and he spent most of it at Yankee Stadium, watching the Yanks demolish any team that had the bad luck to be playing against them. Mickey Mantle. Roger Maris. Whitey Ford on the mound. At least the Dodgers wouldn't be around anymore for them to beat up at World Series time. Not the Brooklyn Dodgers, anyway. They were ancient history now, part of the sad, nostalgic mist that hung around Bedford Avenue and environs these days.

I spent much of the time playing with my two girls, reading them animal stories at bedtime, and catching up on my sleep. I didn't expect to hear any more about the Santini business until it ended up in the courts, and I was happy enough with that. As well as things had turned out, I still had regrets about being a part of it. And then, of course, there was the money I was expected to burn.

At the end of the week I got a call from Nick DeMassio. He wanted to see me, and pronto. I didn't even need to hear the words. It was all in his tone.

He was in his office at the Bath Avenue station. No windows, no circulating air. Most of the times when we met there I would find him pacing the floor. Not today. Today he was lounging behind his gunmetal desk drinking what looked -- and almost smelled -- like coffee.

"Espresso," he said, beaming, before I could ask. "There's a new place just a block from here that sells it."

"I see," I said. "And that's why...?"

"Hell, no. There's news."

"Which is?"

"You know the kid -- the chauffeur -- who was gonna knock off Santini and run away with the daughter?"

"I do," I said.

"They had him over at Raymond Street, remember?"

I had to pause before answering. Raymond Street, actually the Raymond Street Jail, was on Ashland Place in Downtown Brooklyn. It was a dark, gothic dungeon where you waited in supreme discomfort before your trial date. I'd had several bad experiences that involved Raymond Street, and the memories had stayed with me. Raymond Street was where I'd first met Arnie Pulaski. He'd been arrested for the murder of a low-life named Joe Shork and for stealing a car belonging to the District Attorney for Kings County. I was hoping he'd get the chair for either offense, but Gino had convinced his parents that I could find the real killer and set him free. I did, eventually, but there have been times these fourteen years since when I wished I hadn't. Before Arnie, I'd jousted with a crooked guard there who wanted me dead in the worst way. That guard was dead now, but the Raymond Street jail was still there. Every now and then, somebody in city government would say that the place needed to be torn down, but it hadn't happened, and now Harry Appolino was one of its inmates. Maria Santini, also awaiting trial, was in the women's facility at the same location.

"Like I was saying," said DeMassio, noticing my inattention. "The Appolino kid was there."

"Was?"

"Somebody broke him out early this morning. One of the guards, I'm told."

"Better check the airports," I said. "LaGuardia and Idlewild both. Maybe even Newark. It's the fastest way out of the country."

"No need," said DeMassio, grinning now like the Cheshire cat in *Alice in Wonderland*. "Maybe an hour ago a fishing boat on Gravesend Bay found the kid floating. And with his severed dick stuck in his throat. That sound familiar?"

"Jesus," I said.

"Yup. Any time you start thinkin' poor old Jimmy Santini is losin' his killer's edge, you think about this. First Rocco Gabriano, and now his cousin. They both ravished Santini's sweet little daughter, and they've ended up exactly the same for that little indiscretion."

"You're sure it was Santini?" I asked, but I already knew the answer.

"Yup. First he pays money to spring the kid, and then he takes his revenge when the kid is cut loose. I bet he's sittin' up there in that walled castle o' his right now, drinkin' Chianti and thinkin' *he's* still the victim in this crazy business. But really, he's the same as he ever was. A stone killer."

"Jesus," I said.

"There's an upside to all this, of course," said DeMassio, the grin growing still larger.

"And that is?"

"If she's acquitted, sweet little Maria's got two reasons instead of one to come after Daddy again. And this time she might actually pull it off."

"I wouldn't be surprised," I said.

"About?"

"Either possibility."

"You did too good a job, Eddie," said DeMassio dryly. "Santini's still breathin'."

"Anything else you want to blame me for?"

"Well, you did help us snare the wicked stepmother, even if you missed on the shrink as a blackmailer."

"I figured the daughter had made that up," I said, grinning back at him. "She's creative that way. But what about his connection to Brent, the forger?"

"There isn't one...yet."

"But Rothberg owned the building, and my new snitch thinks that..."

"Rosario?"

That stopped me. "You know about him, too?" I asked.

"Uh huh." DeMassio smiled and took a slow, deliberate sip of his espresso.

"All right," I said. "Answer this: how did Santini's daughter know about the print shop? How did she know she could get phony paperwork there if Rothberg didn't tell her?"

"Beats me," said DeMassio. "But the lady *is* a bona fide member of a Mob family, not to mention a criminal organization. She'd know lots of stuff like that."

"So what happens now?"

"This guy Brent, so far, he's not talking, and Rothberg claims he didn't know a damn thing about any illegal activity at the print shop. But, not to worry. I got a feeling if we offer Brent a lighter sentence, he'll rat on Rothberg and we'll have the shrink, too. Not too shabby, huh? Four out of seven from Santini's list. Think about that."

"I'm thinking," I said, glowering at him.

"And think of all that money you saved Santini so he can donate it to the starving children of Africa."

"I don't think that's likely to happen," I said.

"Neither do I, Eddie," said DeMassio, sipping his espresso. "But miracles *can* happen."

"I've heard that before, too."

"So. Any regrets?"

"Santini's still out there. That doesn't sit well."

"Life ain't fair, is it?" said DeMassio, deadpan.

"Amen to that."

"We'll get him," said DeMassio. "One of these days, we'll get him. Or maybe he'll do us all a favor and get himself. Guys like Santini, they always find a way to self-destruct. It's in the genes."

"I hope so," I said.

DeMassio stood up, his broad hint that our conversation was over. "Well, that's the story," he said. "Case closed, right?"

I eyeballed him. "Not quite. What about Enrico Rosario? How did you know he was working for me?"

DeMassio's smile grew until it almost reached his ears. "That's privileged information," he said.

29

I had a few things on my mind when I left DeMassio's office. Part of me wanted to go straight to Nero's and drink myself into a stupor. I'd helped Jimmy Santini to kill somebody. Not exactly an altar boy, but somebody. As much as I tried to dismiss the thought, it kept coming back to me. And, in a way, Arnie's Marine buddy, that was my fault, too. He'd still be alive now if I hadn't hired him. So much for believing that surveillance jobs couldn't hurt you. What turned me away from Nero's finally, and back toward home, was thinking about my girls. Their father did dangerous work, and his employers were not always the best of men. I needed my daughters to keep reminding me what the best of men were supposed to be like.

Anyway, it was over now. At least, I thought it was over. I was eating a late lunch at the kitchen table when I got a call from Watusi. Viper, aka Aabidullah, whom I'd paid off weeks ago, was still in town. He shouldn't have been.

"He's still gunning for me, then?" I asked.

"In a manner of speaking," said Watusi, and I could almost see the odd expression forming at his end of the line.

"I'm missing something here, Tooss," I said.

"Indeed you are," was his answer. "I think you should come for a visit."

"Now?"

"No time like the present," he said, and hung up.

I was almost hoping that the locals would set fire to my Chrysler station wagon when I parked outside Watusi's apartment on West 131st Street so I could pretend I was still single and put a down payment on a Corvette. When Watusi had lived in Harlem, near 125th Street, I'd had several cars destroyed by the locals. I was a white man, I was on their turf, and that was all they needed to know. Spanish Harlem was relatively safer, but I was still hopeful that some harm would come to the Chrysler and I could buy a Chevy again. If not a Corvette, at least a Chevy wagon.

When Watusi met me at the door, I heard sounds from the back of the apartment. Children's voices. Watusi could see that my curiosity had been tweaked, but he said nothing.

"Got guests?" I asked.

"Aabidullah's two sons, Muhammad and Elijah. And their father, of course. Aabidullah's wife, Constance, is out shopping."

"Named one after you, did he?"

"I'm also the boy's godfather. Both boys, actually."

"And Viper –– Aabidullah –– he's still here. Why?"

"He's the best person to answer that question."

"And I damn well plan to ask him," I said, just as Aabidullah walked casually into the room.

"Good afternoon," he said. The sound of the words startled me. It was almost like the sound of a white man speaking, but then I realized that it was the lack of anger in the voice that made it sound that way. His look was calmer as well, and I wondered if Watusi had been right all along; that the angry black man named Viper Robinson no longer existed. But he *had* existed back at Talley's, and almost every word he'd spoken to me there had had venom in it. That was before he'd gone to work for me on the Santini business, of course. Had that been the catalyst for the change I saw and heard in him now? I wasn't sure how to read him, so I answered in a tone that was both cold and remote.

"You're still here," I said. "I thought you were planning to leave the city. You have your money."

"*Earned*," he said, and I heard some of my own coldness in the response.

"True enough," I answered. "Well-earned, even. I don't have any complaints about the work."

"But you want to know why I haven't moved on, scurried way, fled the scene. Am I correct?"

"I suppose so."

"*First*," he said, and there was some bristle in it, "I do not leave a place because some white man expects me to. And I am even more reluctant to go when one *tells* me to. Are you telling me to?"

"No," I said.

"And if I *choose* to stay, for whatever reason, that would be none of your white man's business, would it?"

His look had hardened enough that I could almost see Viper Robinson looking at me through Aabidullah's eyes. "It would damn well be my business if..." I began, but he cut me off.

"If I still wanted you dead. If I were, as they say, still gunning for you."

"Are you?" I asked.

He offered a smile that I couldn't read, then shared it with Watusi before turning away, toward the back of the building. "Are you ready, Muhammad?" he shouted, and when a boy's voice answered, he turned back to me and said quickly, "I'm not gunning for you anymore, but my oldest son apparently is."

As he said it, a lean, tall boy of about ten years entered the room. He was grinning. His left arm was behind his back. He walked toward me, his smile broadening with each step. When he was right in front of me, the hidden arm came into view. There was a small black pistol in his hand, a sight that startled me until I realized that the gun was plastic and probably filled with water. He looked up at his father, his gun at the ready. His father smiled back broadly.

"You have to ask Mr. Lombardi if it's all right, Muhammad," he said. "Not me."

For the first time since I'd arrived at Watusi's, I smiled. It was probably also the first time I'd ever smiled at Aabidullah. I looked at the boy. "What you got in there -- lemonade?"

"No, sir, just water."

"Probably better," I said. "Lemonade would sting."

The boy waited. Aabidullah waited. Watusi waited.

"Fire away," I said, and I got a face full. I smiled at the boy, and then I smiled at Aabidullah. "Well, I guess that's that," I said. I shook the boy's free hand. "Glad to meet you, Muhammad," I said. "I'm

Eddie Lombardi, but I guess you already know that." My next words were for Aabidullah. "Far be it from me to tell you what to do. Like you said, it's none of my white man's business."

He smiled. "Do I get to call you Edward now, or will you still answer to 'cracker' or 'honkey'?"

"Anything but wop or mackerel snapper," I said, returning the smile. "And please, not White Boy."

Another little boy entered the room. He ran right up to me and stood next to his brother. "You must be Elijah," I said. "Your godfather and I are very good friends." I shook his hand, and the boys ran off toward Watusi's garden.

"My wife should be back soon," said Aabidullah. "We found an apartment a few blocks away, near Strivers Row. I found work at a flower shop on 137th Street. Watusi knows the man who owns the place."

"I'd like very much to meet your wife," I said.

He held out his hand to me. "We never tried to do this when we were in the mood for it." And we shook on that.

30

The drive back from Watusi's left me perplexed. Had it really been that easy to transform years of animosity and suspicion into something that almost seemed to resemble friendship? Watusi's one great love, Alma, had been the unintended cause of it all, and I knew she must be smiling down on us now knowing that the bitterness her death had caused us had finally come to an end. A moment of forlorn optimism made me think that maybe all of it could change somehow, that there would no longer be niggers or honkeys anywhere, that hate could be banished back into its ugly box. A box that would never again be opened. But it was just a moment of false hope, and nothing more.

My mind turned back to Jimmy Santini. A reality check, a look at the world the way it really was. The world that my two children would grow up in. I remembered telling Laura before we married that our kids, as yet unborn, would never live in fear of Santini or anybody like him. I would teach them to see things as they were, and they would rise above it all somehow. It was harder to get my head around that idea now than it ever had been. I had helped Santini before without actually being in his employ. Back in '47. That was different. But when he'd told me to actually hire on this time, I'd done it. Part of it was necessity, and part of that necessity was fear. The same fear that I'd told my children would never rule their lives. Maybe it would have been better if the chauffeur and Santini's daughter hadn't failed, if Santini was the only one dead at the end of this nasty business; but that didn't sit right, either. Murder is murder, no matter who's on the receiving end. Nobody, not even Jimmy Santini, deserved that. Maybe Nick DeMassio was right. In time, maybe somebody else would finally get to him. Another mobster, maybe, or some bimbo he'd crossed somehow, or another wife. Maybe even the Barracuda Brothers would sour on him enough to perform that service. Occupational hazard. Domestic violence. Patricide. I, for one, would never work for him again, no matter what the reason. I needed to learn the lesson I thought I'd already taught to my kids.

I took a long detour on the way home and stopped off at St. John Cemetery in Queens to see if the stone marker for Aurelio was in place. It wasn't. I'd call the guy I'd hired to make the monument as soon as I got back to the office. I lingered only a moment at the grave, not long enough to respect all that he'd done for me, albeit grudgingly, and for money. Nowhere near long enough for that, but I thought about him as I drove back to Bensonhurst, listening to the cylinders misfire on the Chrysler. He'd had nobody in his life, nobody at all. Maybe that was why J.T.S. Brown had been his best friend. More regret there that we could never be real friends because of who and what he was, and because of who and what I was. A missed opportunity that I wouldn't have the chance to rectify.

I stopped downstairs at the Bella Italia Luncheonette to get a copy of the *Daily News* and a cold Coke, then trudged up the narrow stairs to my office. Lacking activity, the room, as always, looked a bit smaller. There had been no calls at the answering service, so there was nothing to do. Arnie Pulaski was probably chasing the girls again, hopefully one less lethal than Maria Santini. Liam was, no doubt, almost completely recovered at his place in Midwood, flipping through the colorful pages of the latest girlie magazine. *Wild Vixen*, or *Hot Babes*, or something similar. I opened the paper to the Sports section. There was a new baseball team coming, not to Brooklyn, but Queens. They were called the Metropolitan Baseball Club -- the Mets. They were going to be in the National League, and they'd be playing at the old Polo Grounds in Upper Manhattan until they had a proper stadium of their own built out in Flushing Meadows. I didn't think much about the news. No team could ever replace the Dodgers in Brooklyn's heart of hearts, and nothing could replace the emptiness their exit had brought about.

The longer I sat in the office, the more my mood deteriorated. I wondered where Frankie DeFilippo might be at this moment. Angelo might know, but I decided to go straight to Frankie's place of business and find out for myself. I needed a haircut anyway. Happily, the barber pole outside was lit. I opened the door and walked in. There was a March of Dimes jar on a small table next to the door. I usually put in the mandatory deposit of a quarter on the way out, but Frankie gestured in that direction and scowled, so I put in my two bits early. He was working on giving Old Mr. Saladino a shave, so I took a chair and picked up a copy of *Life*. Liz Taylor was on the cover. When Frankie was finished with Old Mr. Saladino, he bid him good afternoon, swept up around the barber chair, and finally gave me some attention.

"Eddie. What's up?" he said.

"I should be asking *you*," I answered. "Could have used you on a surveillance a couple of weeks back."

"I was out of town," he said.

"Probably a good thing. The guy I hired in place of you got shot dead in a phone booth. So, where the hell were you? Even Angelo didn't know."

"Atlantic City," he said.

"Oh."

"You here for a haircut? I got an appointment in fifteen minutes, but I could probably squeeze you in."

"Sure," I said, and sat in the barber chair.

"They got Monopoly streets down there in Atlantic City. Did you know that?"

"No," I said. "Never did."

"Sure enough. Marvin Gardens, Atlantic Avenue, Baltic, St. Charles, Park Place, Mediterranean. All o' those."

I grinned. "Went to play Monopoly, did you?"

"Went with a girl."

"Surprise, surprise. And how old was this one?"

"Well, she said twenty-two, but she might have been a little younger."

"Beware of jail bait, my friend," I said.

"She wasn't no jail bait. Stacked like the Queen Mary, she was. And affectionate, if you know what I mean."

192

"Remind me to keep you far away from my daughters. Look at you, *paisano*, past forty and still on the prowl like some horny teenager. Why don't you find some nice, forty-year-old librarian lady and settle down?"

"I like the thrill of the chase, not the catch," he said. "When I land 'em, I gotta throw 'em back in."

"What was wrong with this one?" I asked.

"She gambled," he said with a deadpan look.

I let him cut my hair, and we exchanged the usual small talk and gossip. It was so good, seeing him again, that I even put a second quarter in the March of Dimes jar on the way out. And as I walked back home to the wife and kids, to our house on 16th Avenue, I felt a little better. For a moment, I didn't quite know why, but then I did. As crazy as this world could be, as corrupt and ugly and disappointing, I knew that as long as there were straight-up guys like Frankie DeFilippo living in it, there was room for optimism.

In my newfound optimism, I figured that my official day was done. There were just a few things to finish up back at the office, but I could take care of those without too much difficulty, and then I could go home to my family. I even had a new book picked out to read to the kids: *Alice in Wonderland*. Having been down the rabbit hole myself, it would be easy work.

But I was wrong about the optimism.

Gino's daughter Gloria was waiting outside my office with her latest boyfriend. She was wearing a white dress shirt with the tails out, blue jeans with the cuffs rolled up, and open-toed sandals without socks. Her hair, set in a pageboy, was in disarray. The boyfriend didn't look Puerto Rican. He was, in fact, almost a blonde. I unlocked the office door, opened it, and they followed. I smiled briefly at both of them, but Gloria scowled back.

"My father hired you to follow me," she said, pouting. "Well, didn't he?"

"He tried to," I said.

"But he *wanted* you to follow me."

"Yes."

"Why?"

"You'll have to take that up with him," I said.

"He doesn't like my friends, he doesn't like the way I look. He doesn't like one thing about me."

"Not my business," I said, and walked to my desk. The chair squeaked when I sat in it. It was a comfort to me, but a small one.

"He is *so* square," she said, the look intensifying.

"A father's prerogative," I answered.

"Well, he doesn't *own* me."

"In a way, he does," I said. "Unless you're paying for your own tuition up there at NYU."

"This is Gregorio," she said, pointing at her friend. "He's from Spain. He's a poet. His poems have four-letter words, because four-letter words need to be spoken. They're important."

I nodded in the young man's direction. I offered a polite smile, but I really wanted to be home.

"So, are you still going to follow me?" she asked. "Spy on me? Rat me over to my father?"

"I never really started," I said. "But if you'd like me to, I charge fifty dollars a day, plus expenses."

"Very funny, Eddie."

"You used to call me Uncle Eddie. You used to sit on my lap and giggle. You had manners then."

"Why are adults *so* square?" she said, looking at her boyfriend with intensity.

"Maybe because they've grown up," I said. "Come back and see me when *you* have."

I didn't watch them when they left, but I heard Gloria stomping her feet all the way down the stairs. I left the office a few minutes after I was sure they were gone, forgetting whatever it was that I'd planned to do in the office. Then, as if to offer another blow to my fading optimism, it started to rain again. A cold, biting rain, and an omen.

The times were changing, all right. The man who called himself Malcolm X was a part of it, and the Beat Generation was another. I wondered if my two girls could fit into the brave -- or not so brave -- new world that was coming. I wondered if I could. I wondered if it was worth the effort.

But then I thought about *Alice in Wonderland*, and Alice, and the Mad Hatter, and the Cheshire cat, and the smoking caterpillar, and the Queen of Hearts, and I knew that my two little girls would love every word of it. And they would love the father who read the story to them every night.

But before that, I would light a fire in the fireplace.

A very expensive fire.